NT

eting
re in
met
own,
each man pacing slowly in the face of death. Only one would walk away. The town held its breath and watched as one of the greatest gunfighters of all time fell on his face in the dust. The other walked away.

More Blade Westerns
In Hamlyn Paperbacks

THE INDIAN INCIDENT
THE TUCSON CONSPIRACY

THE LAREDO ASSIGNMENT

Matt Chisholm

Hamlyn Paperbacks

THE LAREDO ASSIGNMENT

ISBN 0 600 31485 5

First published in Great Britain 1979
by Hamlyn Paperbacks

Hamlyn Paperbacks are published by
The Hamlyn Publishing Group Ltd,
Astronaut House,
Feltham,
Middlesex, England

Set, printed and bound in Great Britain by
Cox & Wyman Ltd,
London, Reading and Fakenham

I

As the parson said – there is nothing like a little sin to cheer a man up.

When Big Jim Flaherty needed cheering up, he rode into Laredo and put a few drinks under his belt. After that he went sinning for a few days and nights among those ladies of the town known as soiled doves. Maybe that cheered him up and maybe it did not. We shall never know, for, when next he walked out on to the streets of Laredo, he was shot dead.

Eyewitnesses saw a man ride his horse alongside Big Jim and shoot him dead with one well-placed shot. The murderer then laughed and rode out of town.

These eyewitnesses, some of whom possibly were not too sober themselves, all swore that the killer was a Mexican. But that was about all they ever did agree on. The Anglos among them said it was a goddam greaser, a low *pelado* type, the worst kind there was. Some said he was tall, some short, some young, some not so young. The Mexicans said that he was possibly a Mexican or maybe he was an Anglo dressed as a Mexican. That was a typical gringo trick, so that the blame for the crime would not fall on an Anglo.

And maybe it was after all a real Mexican, because Laredo was about as close to Mexico as it could get without actually being in the land of tortillas and señoritas. Nobody would deny that Laredo was a natural jumping-off place for badmen south of the Border who wanted to raise a little hell to the north of it. So when some of the witnesses said they were pretty sure the killer was a Mexican, nobody thought to argue about it.

Which meant nobody would be punished for the killing, because naturally whoever was guilty had slipped away back below the Border to safety. So what few law-men there were in those parts made no fuss.

Right from the start it was a strange affair. None of it made much sense, mainly because nobody could imagine that anybody would want Big Jim dead. He did not have an enemy in the world, or so men said around the saloons in town. Maybe, they added, that Mex killed him for no goddam reason at all, just out of sheer cussedness. Who, I ask you, could tell what a Mex would do next? No more than you could tell what an Indian would do, either.

The strangest thing of all, though, was that Ransome S. Howard hired Joe Blade to find the killers for him – in confidence. Which meant that he did not want anybody to know what he had hired Blade for. And neither Joe Blade nor anybody else would have been able to guess at any connection between Ransome S. Howard and Jim Flaherty.

The pay was good and the risk seemed minimal – at any rate at first. Blade would have been a fool not to accept the offer.

Just the same . . .

At Howard's vast house in Kansas City, Kansas, in the large study hung with paintings supposedly of Howard's ancestors, Blade asked: 'Why do you want to know who killed Flaherty, Mr Howard?'

Howard replied: 'The simple answer to that, Blade, is that it is none of your business. No offence meant. When a man is willing to pay your excessive charges, it does not seem to me to be too much to ask for confidential work and for silence on the subject. What possible reason can you have for wanting to know why I wish to hire you?'

Blade had to admit that Howard was not unreasonable. But he did not like the man's attitude just the same.

He asked: 'Is or was Flaherty related to you in any way?'

Howard was a small man of nervous temperament, mercurial

nature, a successful man's high opinion of himself and a quick temper. That temper was backed solidly by a good many million dollars. Blade was reminded of a carefully shaven prairie dog.

Howard said sharply: 'Are you incapable of investigating a murder without delving into my relations? All I am asking and paying through the nose for is for you to find the man who killed Flaherty. I don't want to find out anything about myself or anybody but Flaherty's killer. That's what I'm hiring you for.'

'From what you tell me,' Blade said, 'a solitary Mexican rode up alongside Big Jim and simply shot him. Are you in any way sure it happened like that? Was it a drunken Mexican who was shooting off his gun? Are we even sure it was murder?' He tucked his hands into the pockets of his neat fawn pants and looked calmly at the excitable and wealthy man in front of him.

'If that is so,' Howard snapped, 'why do you want to know the relationship between Flaherty and me?'

Blade said: 'It would not occur to me, Mr Howard, to tell you your business. Judging by your bank balance you do pretty well at it. I do pretty well in my line of business and my bank balance is pretty healthy, too. When I tell you I shall have to dig around to do what you want, it would be good business to listen. The more digging I do, the more you pay. If you don't give me the information, I'll have to dig for it and you'll have to pay later. In cash.'

The little man swallowed and his eyes bulged a little.

He didn't like this, either, being asked for information, or the tone Blade used. He said: 'There's no connection between Flaherty and me. Flaherty and I. You will not waste time looking for one. Is that understood?'

Blade nodded.

'That'll be two hundred dollars in advance,' he said.

Howard showed genuine shock.

'What?' he said. 'An advance? What is this?'

'It's customary,' Blade said.

'You mean my credit is not good with you?' cried Howard, rising from behind his desk. 'A hundred reputable businessmen accept my word and a man of your kind has the audacity to doubt it?'

Blade said: 'I'm a businessman, Mr Howard. My experience has taught me that wealthy men are bad payers. If I did not learn from experience, I would go out of business. Either I'm paid or you look elsewhere for somebody to solve the mystery of Flaherty's death.'

Howard's small knuckles banged down on the desk top.

'You're insolent, sir,' he cried.

'But solvent,' said Blade.

Howard stared at him for a moment, then sat down. He picked up a small silver bell and rang it. A grey man entered the room almost at once, as though he had been hovering outside the door awaiting a summons. Blade smiled to himself; Howard plainly did not do anything so mundane as actually handle money.

Howard said: 'Pay this man two hundred dollars and see him out.'

The grey man inspected Blade with solemn eyes and said softly: 'You will be good enough to come this way, sir?'

Blade turned to Howard – 'I shall make my first report one week from now.'

Howard ignored him. Blade followed the grey man from the room. They paced together down a corridor and entered another room. This one did not possess a carpet. Just bare boards, a small desk, and shelves with papers piled on them.

The grey man went to a large safe and drew out money. While he counted it, Blade asked: 'Was Jim Flaherty kin to Ransome S. Howard?'

The grey man completed his counting, muttered a number

under his breath, raised his eyes, gave Blade a hooded look and said: 'I'm sorry, sir, I know of no Jim Flaherty. May I ask what name I shall write on the receipt?'

'Joseph Santiago Blade.'

'Thank you, sir.'

The name was scratched in fine copper plate writing. Blade signed for the money. Above his name was written – 'For services rendered.'

Blade pocketed the money.

'Do you know what those services are?' Blade asked.

The man looked at the floor.

'No, sir. I have no idea. I imagine they are confidential. Had Mr Howard wished me to know of them, he would have told me himself. Now, I shall show you out.'

'That's all right, Mr Chard,' said a voice from the door. 'I'll do that.'

Blade turned.

She stood in the open doorway. The sunlight coming through the window caught her red hair. The startlingly green eyes were enough to stop a man in his tracks. The rest of her was the best that any eighteen-year-old girl could offer.

The grey man said: 'Miss June, I don't think that Mr Howard would approve.'

'Mr Howard,' said the girl, 'won't know.'

She turned and gestured for Blade to follow her. He thanked the grey man and left the room. She led the way to the stairs without so much as glancing at him. Blade was under the impression that she wanted to get him past Howard's study door.

At the foot of the stairs in the centre of the great shining hall with its ornate mirrors and expanse of paintings, she stopped and said: 'I'm June Howard. What is your name, sir?'

'Blade, Miss Howard. Joseph Blade.'

'And what is your business, Mr Blade?'

She was very tall, nearly the same height as Blade. But she was perfectly proportioned, filling her green suit admirably, dressed demurely enough, but quite unable to conceal the proclamation of a beautiful body beneath.

'My own, Miss Howard.'

She flushed. The green eyes seemed to darken in their anger. But there was a reason for her not being openly angry with him. So she controlled her anger. Blade could see that she was that kind of woman. No more than eighteen, but very much a woman. The eyes told of experience, and of a woman who felt deeply. This was no sheltered rich girl.

'You are perhaps a little insolent, Mr Blade,' she said very softly. The rebuke was like a sensual caress.

Blade smiled ever so faintly.

'Mr Howard thought the same,' he said.

She went on towards the front door, entering the small lobby and turning to him again.

'You make me curious, Mr Blade,' she said. 'My father hires some strange men, off and on, but they don't usually come here. When they do they are not invited through the front entrance.'

Blade's smile was cold now.

'Maybe he thought he could pass me off as a gentleman, ma'am,' he said.

'You look to be a very secret man, Mr Blade,' she said. She was standing very close and her voice was low. There was an intimacy in her manner that got to him and he could wish that he knew this girl under other circumstances. Her subtle scent entered his nostrils and teased his masculinity. 'My father prides himself on holding information to himself. I imagine you both over-estimate yourselves. Men invariably do, don't they?'

With mock indulgence, Blade said: 'I didn't expect to find an advocate of woman's rights in the house of Ransome S. Howard.'

'I'm an advocate of woman's strength,' she said. 'Will you not change your mind, sir, and tell me your business?'

'Maybe I have no business, Miss Howard,' he said. 'Possibly I am a gentleman of leisure.'

She laughed almost silently.

'In that case, my father would have nothing to do with you,' she said. 'He is all business. Gentility is frivolous, or didn't you know?'

She opened the front door.

He gave her a small bow and said: 'Goodbye, Miss Howard. It has been a great pleasure to meet you. I could only wish that there could be the greater pleasure of our meeting again.'

She smiled – or perhaps grinned would have been a better word. She grinned at him like a gamine, her eyes suddenly full of taunt and promise.

'I do believe you really meant that polite phrase, Mr Blade,' she told him. 'If you did, I wouldn't be surprised if you had that greater pleasure before long.'

'I doubt it, ma'am, much as I may regret it,' he said. 'I am off on my travels.'

'To Laredo,' she said.

It was a statement.

He kept his face expressionless, but she had shaken him.

'Little girls,' he said, 'shouldn't listen at keyholes.'

'Little is one thing I am not,' she said. 'My father thinks I am a freak and that at my height no man will so much as look at me.'

'That I can't believe,' he said. 'I haven't stopped looking at you since I first saw you. Should you happen to be in Laredo . . .'

She was grinning again. Now there was a kind of controlled hunger in the grin.

She said: 'You know, Mr Blade, I think maybe you're a very nice man.'

He bowed and started away down the steps between the two

great white pillars – 'Nice is hardly the word I would use, Miss Howard, but it's kind of you to use it.'

She leaned against the door-jamb and her full body curved delightfully inside the green costume.

'Would you say I was nice, Mr Blade?'

'Again,' he said, 'nice is hardly the right word.'

'What is the right word, Mr Blade?'

'It's a long trip to Laredo, Miss Howard,' he replied. 'I could not be better employed in searching for the right one. If I were to see you in Laredo and if you were to indicate that I might call on you there, that would give me the opportunity of telling you.'

She laughed deep in her throat.

'Do that, Mr Blade,' she said. 'Yes, I think nice is the right word. Maybe a few more words as well, but nice will do for now.'

He strode away down the long drive. When he looked back, she was still standing there, watching him.

When he reached his hotel, the desk clerk told him: 'Mr Blade, there was a man here asking for you.'

'Did he leave a name?'

'No, sir.'

The clerk said that the man had been small and dark, unremarkable. He wore a plainsman's hat and a brown store-bought suit, cattleman's boots. Aged thirty-five or thereabouts. Moustache. Spoke with a Southern drawl. Could have been anybody. Blade climbed the stairs to his room. When he had lit the lamp, he saw that he had been visited in his absence.

2

It wasn't the first time in his life that he'd had his room searched. It was an occupational hazard in his profession. Just the same, it never failed to leave him with a strange chill down his spine. And it always angered him.

This time, the searcher or searchers had worked fast and had not cared how much damage they did. It was as if their need to find something was reinforced by a personal hatred for him. They had used knives and ripped up everything that could be ripped. The destruction had given them pleasure. The lining of his grip had been slashed and torn out. Every seam of his clothing seemed to have been opened. They had even ripped the lining from his gun case in which his silver-mounted Colt 1859s were kept. They were obsolete weapons, but treasured examples of the best of the gunmaker's art. They had been given to him by Charles Goodnight as a token of his gratitude for what Blade had considered a trifling act of generosity. He greatly admired the pioneer cattleman and had not wished to take money from him.

'How about the guns, you damn young fool?' Charles Goodnight had said. 'Will you take the guns?' And Blade had not been able to refuse. His collector's instinct was too strong in him. The great rancher had laughed in his dry ironic way and said: 'Every man has his price.'

Blade sat on the bed amongst the debris and gazed at the beautiful, ruined case.

'The bastards,' he said softly.

Then he began the long, detailed check to see if they had

taken anything. An hour later, he reckoned they had taken nothing. The fact did not surprise him, because there wasn't anything to take – anything, that was, that he could think of. One thing for sure: they had not been after money. Men didn't make this kind of search for money. These fellows had been looking for something small and flat.

He allowed himself a drink now and started tidying the place. By the time a clock somewhere struck midnight, he was ready for bed and he had erased his anger from his mind.

He lay back on the bed with his hands behind his head, fully dressed and thinking about June Howard. They were good thoughts and he enjoyed them. She was a fine girl and she made even Laredo seem worthwhile. He could not help wondering how a dried up old goat like her father could have sired such loveliness. Her mother must have been a peach.

He had started to doze when a light tap came on the door.

Not surprisingly, he had turned the key in the lock.

'Who's this?' he asked.

'It's the desk clerk, Mr Blade.'

He recognised the voice.

'What is it?' he asked.

'A letter has been delivered to you by hand, sir.'

Blade sat up. He reached under the pillow and fetched out the tiny Remington derringer, two barrels, up-and-over. Close up, it could blow a hole in a man you could drive a coach and horses through. He slipped it into his silk vest pocket.

'Who brought it?' he demanded.

'The same man who called earlier, sir.'

'Slip it under the door.'

There was a slight pause before the man said: 'It's too fat, sir. It's a kind of package.'

Blade stood up and slipped the little gun from his pocket. Holding it against his leg, he stepped to the door and turned the key with his left hand.

It all happened very quickly then.

Even before he had turned the door handle, a great weight was hurled against the door and it burst open. Blade tried to step back and avoid it, but it crashed into him so violently that he was almost knocked from his feet.

The club hit him with sickening impact across the face.

As he went down, his right hand automatically raised the derringer, but another blow stretched him on the floor. He was shocked and dazed, but still conscious. He saw the guns in the two men's hands and he knew they were both cocked. He knew that he was very close to death.

Through his half-focussed eyes, he saw the desk clerk being thrown into the room and clubbed to the floor. The fellow lay there groaning and whimpering.

One of the men sat on the bed and watched him. He was a big fellow with a florid face, all muscle and bone with narrow lips and flat belly. One day he would run to fat, but now he was in the peak of condition.

The other fellow turned a chair the wrong way around, sat on it and stared at Blade over the back. This was the man who had asked for him earlier. The wide-brimmed hat, the brown suit and the cowman's boots.

Both men held their guns like men who were used to handling them.

'All right, Blade,' said the man in the brown suit, 'where is it?'

The head of the club had clipped Blade's mouth. The upper lip had been mashed against his teeth. Luckily, the teeth were still intact. Just the same, talking was neither easy nor comfortable.

'Where's what?' he said.

The man on the bed rolled his eyes to heaven.

'Oh, Jesus,' said the man on the bed, 'he's going to waste our time.' He spoke with all the fervour of a religious fanatic.

The man in the brown suit admonished him with a sad glance.

'No, he's not,' he said. 'He's too smart for that. He knows the kind we are. You know what kind we are, don't you, Blade? You're a professional like us, aren't you? You know the score. You know there's no profit in foolin' with our kind, because we know how to do horrible things to you.'

The desk clerk groaned and tried to sit up. He put his face in his hands and blood seeped out between his fingers.

'You've broken my head,' he said indistinctly. 'I'll bleed to death. My God, I'm going to die.'

The man in the brown suit chuckled.

'You do enjoy your work,' he told the man on the bed.

'I got to admit it,' said the big man. 'I'm real dedicated. When I hit a man, he stays hit.'

Blade said: 'You boys shouldn't hang around. You made a hell of a racket. Somebody had to hear you and raise the alarm.'

'That's true,' said the brown suit. 'Which means we have to work fast. So we work fast. And you know what that means, Blade. We have to make you talk quick.'

Blade sat up.

'Don't sit up,' said the brown suit. 'Stay flat on the floor. I prefer you that way.'

Blade looked at the gun pointed at his heart and obeyed.

Brown suit said: 'Don't get between Blade and me, pardner. Use the knife. They always come around fast to my way of thinkin' when you start on the fingernails. I learned that from the Cheyenne when I wasn't no more'n a button. Real dandy at it, they was. Used little wooden splinters.'

The big man rose from the bed and the springs twanged unmusically. He put his gun away in his coat pocket and produced a large clasp knife. He opened the blade and nodded amiably at his potential victim.

'This is goin' to hurt you more'n it hurts me,' he said. 'An' then some.'

The desk clerk said: 'I'll bleed to death. I got to have a doctor.'

'Five minutes at the outside,' said the brown suit, 'an' every doc in the city will be at your disposal, my friend.'

The big man edged around behind Blade. He smelled of cattle and sweat. His knee joint cracked as he got down on one knee.

'Give me your left hand,' he said. 'I always start with the left. It seems to be lucky.'

'No,' said Blade, 'don't do it. I don't have anything to tell you.'

Brown suit said: 'Have a last little think, friend. Just tell us where you have it hid an' we'll go. It'll be all over, an' just like it never happened. My word on it.'

'All right,' said Blade, 'I'll tell you. I know I couldn't stand the pain.'

'You're smart,' said the big man.

Blade reached up and caught him by his long black hair, wrenching his face forward and down.

Instinctively, the man in the brown suit fired.

The roar of the gun in the small room was deafening. At once the air was full of the powerfully acrid smell of burned powder. Blade was conscious of it as he made his next move.

The big man was hurled backward as the heavy ball thudded into him with a sound like the breaking of a gigantic egg.

Blade's right hand slapped down on to the tiny gun he had dropped when he fell. It seemed that he watched for an age as the man in the brown suit pulled back the hammer of his gun.

Blade fired a fraction of a second before the other.

The face of the man in the brown suit showed utter surprise and shock as the chair teetered back on two legs. Then man and chair hit the floor and the building seemed to shake to its foundations. Before the man landed, Blade had fired a second time.

Plaster rained down from the ceiling as the dead man's shot ploughed into it.

Blade stayed where he was, gasping. The fumes from the gun hit him and he started coughing. He thought he would never stop coughing.

He heard a sound.

The frightened face of a man in his night-shirt showed in the doorway.

'Fetch a doctor,' Blade said and heard the tremor in his own voice. 'Fast.'

The desk clerk was weeping. Blade couldn't blame him. He felt a bit like weeping himself.

My God, he thought, *the price of Ransome S. Howard's assignment just went up.*

After that there was some trouble for a couple of hours and it was in the lap of the gods whether he ended up in the Kansas City jail in the middle of the night or not. The city marshal wavered between treating him like a common criminal who had murdered two innocent men or a hero who had saved the life of an inoffensive hotel clerk. In the end, the clerk's evidence weighed the balance in his favour. Blade could go, but he must not leave town.

He walked across town to the Howard mansion. The gravel of the drive crunched richly under his feet and the distant bell rang as he tugged at the bell-pull.

The butler looked like a debauched quaker.

'Yes?'

'I'd like to see Mr Howard.'

'I fear that Mr Howard is not at home.' If somebody had told Blade that this fellow was Great Britain's ambassador to the United States, he would have believed it.

'Just the same, tell him Blade is here to see him.'

The man looked somewhat aghast. His eyes were as scandalised as an insulted nun's. He looked down his nose and said: 'I have already told you, Mr – er – Blade that Mr Howard is not here. He left town an hour ago. It's very late.'

Blade advanced one step.

'I have to see Mr Howard,' he said. 'It is in his own interest.'

A woman spoke behind the butler. The man turned his head to listen to the words that Blade failed to catch.

The butler said: 'Very well, madam,' then turned back to Blade, his gaze totally disapproving. 'Madam will have a word with you. Come in.' Blade took his hat off and stepped into the lobby. The man said: 'Please follow madam.'

Blade saw June Howard's lovely form going down the vast hall. The lamplight caught the glorious red hair. He reckoned his pulse-rate increased by a good few beats per minute.

Take a grip on yourself, Blade, he told himself. *Remember, you're only the hired help.*

She opened a door at the far end of the hall and entered a room. He followed her and closed the door behind him. There was soft lamplight in here. Her subtle scent hung gently and tantalizingly on the air. She had changed it since he was here last. Maybe this was her night-time choice.

She stood with her back to him and waited for him to speak.

'Is it true,' he asked, 'that he isn't here?'

She turned and said: 'Perfectly true.'

She wasn't June.

She had the same magnificent build, the same challenging body and mocking eyes, the identical red hair, but she wasn't June.

'I'm sorry,' he said, 'I thought you were Miss Howard.'

She was maybe six or seven years older than June. They were six or seven years in her favour. They added charm and other indefinable assets.

'I'm Mrs Howard,' she told him. 'I gather that you are the notorious Joseph Blade.' She smiled as she said it, as if to indicate that she had no wish to sting him. There was a friendly, mocking air about her.

'I'm Joe Blade, ma'am,' he admitted. 'I'm not sure the "notorious" goes down too well.'

He liked her. There were two qualities that showed, seemingly contradictory. One was tranquillity, the other was passion. Yet she was presumably married to Ransome S. Howard. How could one be tranquil or passionate married to a man like that?

Then the idea hit Blade. This was Howard's *second* wife. So the daughter looked like the first wife and Howard had chosen for his second a woman who looked like his first.

'May I say, ma'am,' he said with the politeness of the period, 'that Mr Howard is indeed fortunate to have such charming ladies under the same roof?'

It was a simple compliment, but she liked it.

'You may indeed, Mr Blade,' she said. 'Now, how may I help you? Is there anything I can do in place of Mr Howard?'

There were plenty of answers to that, but Blade was too much of a gentleman to voice them. His mind ran riot for a second or two.

'Will you be seeing him shortly, Mrs Howard?' he asked.

'It's possible.'

He debated with himself how to say what he had to.

'Mr Howard commissioned me earlier this evening to carry out a small task for him,' he said. He decided to make it blunt. It would be interesting to see if this woman's calm could be shaken. 'Since then, there have been some developments. We made an oral contract. That contract no longer holds good because I have discovered that the circumstances are not as described to me by Mr Howard.'

A white hand went up to the long curving throat, a throat that was made to be kissed, not to belong to an old goat like Howard. It seemed a sinful waste of a wonderful looking woman.

She said: 'Are you saying, Mr Blade, that my husband made a contract with you unfairly?'

'The idea has suggested itself, ma'am,' he said.

'Then I would say that you're mistaken, sir,' she said. Her

indignation was all the more magnificent for its being calmly expressed. 'My husband never committed a dishonest act in his life. He has built his business on his integrity.'

'Mr Howard mentioned nothing to me about physical danger, Mrs Howard,' Blade said. 'All he saw fit to mention to me was a simple and straightforward enquiry. The kind of thing that is ordinary day-to-day, bread-and-butter work for a man in my profession. Yet, within an hour or so of our coming to an agreement, my hotel room has been ransacked and two men have attempted to murder me.'

The words hung darkly between them.

'My God,' she said. She was deeply shaken now. 'Were you able to defend yourself?'

'I'm here,' Blade said.

'How stupid of me. Of course. May I ask—?'

Blade hesitated for a moment, then said: 'The two men are dead, ma'am. One accidentally shot the other, and I shot the survivor.'

She was shocked to speechlessness. He felt a little sorry for her as she looked suddenly vulnerable.

She looked at him almost pleadingly – 'And you came here . . . for what?'

'Like your husband, ma'am,' he said, 'I am in business for money. When my life is in danger, the price is somewhat higher than ordinarily.'

Her voice was very soft when she said: 'So now the price has gone up?'

'Considerably, ma'am. If I am to be killed, I want some security for those who depend on me.'

'Of course.'

She was looking at him curiously.

She said: 'I shall tell Mr Howard.'

'Tell him that I shall not go ahead until I get another thousand dollars advance. Tell him also that I'm now aware that he told me only part of the story. And I cannot work in the dark.'

She was silent for a moment and then said: 'I'll tell him this.'

'Tell him also that only one man in Kansas City knew where I was staying and that was him.'

His statement hit her between the eyes. She licked her lips because they were very dry.

'Would you leave now, Mr Blade?' she said.

'Certainly, ma'am,' he said. 'I see that the revulsion has set in. Just remember that it's men like me who carry out the wishes of men like your husband. Indirectly, I pay for this place, for the very expensive but very lovely robe you're wearing.'

'That was unnecessarily brutal, Mr Blade. Please go now.'

'Usually they touch me,' he said, 'to see if I'm like the respectable men they know.' There was not an ounce of expression in his voice. 'I guess you wouldn't touch me if you wore gloves, Mrs Howard.'

A ghastly, strained smile appeared on her face. It took all her effort to put it there.

'You're showing there's a sensitive man under that hard exterior,' she said. 'I'm sorry I was offensive.'

He didn't move.

Slowly, she walked towards him.

When she halted, Blade found that her height almost put her eyes on the same level as his. He reckoned she was about the same height as her step-daughter. But her eyes were not green, they were a deep violet. Blade had never seen such eyes. There was a beguiling warmth in them. Slowly she raised a hand and laid its palm against his face. It was as cool as marble.

He raised his own hand and took hers in it. Then he laid his other hand on top of hers and hid the white flesh with the brown.

'That's not so bad, is it, Mrs Howard?' he said. 'You can always wash it when I'm gone.'

'You mistake me,' she said.

'In what way?'

'I didn't judge you,' she told him. 'I'm not judging you now. You and I come from the same worlds. I didn't grow up with all this.'

He leaned forward and kissed her gently on the base of her neck. She shuddered once and leaned against him. When he put his arms around her, her arms came around his neck. When they kissed, a feeling of utter peace came over him. Then the peace dissolved and turned to fire. But, just the same, it was he who held back.

'I guess that wasn't a very smart thing to do,' he said. 'I don't make a habit of kissing a client's wife at first meeting.'

Her mood changed abruptly. She was suddenly relaxed and at ease with him.

'I hope not, Mr Blade.' Her eyes were laughing.

The door opened and June Howard walked in.

She stopped and stared at them hard. She didn't like what she saw. Her step-mother's hands were in Blade's.

'This doesn't look much like Laredo, Mr Blade,' she said.

'Perceptive of you, Miss Howard,' he said. 'Mrs Howard was kind enough to agree to give a message to Mr Howard for me.'

'If it's about the two men who attacked you in the hotel,' she said, 'there's no need. He already knows.'

3

It is a long way from Kansas City, Kansas, to Laredo, Texas. The distance covered by the railroad seems short enough, all things considered, but the part covered by the stage line seems a hundred times as far as it really is.

When Joe Blade stepped off the stage at Laredo, he wished he'd ridden. His spine felt as if it had penetrated his skull, his backside felt reluctant ever to sit down again. But he was alive and in one piece, if that fact was any consolation.

So he stepped into the half-Texan, half-Mexican world of Laredo and wondered what the place held for him. He lit a stogie to drive away the flies, eased his necktie against the heat, and sought his hotel. This proved to be the Lone Star Hotel and, for the Border, it did not seem half bad. He cleaned up, knocked the dust of the trail from his clothes, and sat down to a meal that seemed to consist mainly of chilis and hot sauce. This brought some more sweat out on him, and the lovely Mexican girl who waited on him promised to bring out a little more still.

There was a Ranger station in town and he found it in the cool of the evening. In the dingy office, he found one Captain Henry McNally.

Blade said: 'Charlie Goodnight said for me to tell you hello, captain. Name's Joe Blade.'

The captain nodded and held out a gnarled hand. Blade knew of him. He was a man who once had a ranch out on the Staked Plain. That was until the Comanches wiped him out.

At the same time, they had wiped out his wife and three kids. After that, he gave up raising cows and joined the Rangers. He'd chased Indians and Mexican bandits ever since. He was something of a legend on the Border. It was said that the bandidos seldom hit Laredo because they knew that the Border would not prevent McNally from following them down into Old Mexico or even to hell and back, no matter what international laws said.

'I heard of you,' he said and offered Blade a drink.

While they drank, Blade said: 'I'm hoping you can give me some information.'

'If I can.'

'I'm hired to find the killer of Big Jim Flaherty.'

The ranger shot him a hard glance from under thick eyebrows.

'I can't tell you a thing about it,' he said. 'All I know is a heap of folks say they saw a Mex shoot him. The description of the Mex differs a little more than somewhat. There don't seem any rhyme or reason to it. Maybe the feller was boozin', got kind of wild and shot the first white man he came on. It happens. Who can tell what a Mex will do next?'

Blade gave a thought to his own Mexican mother.

'I don't know about that,' he said. 'I want to know about Jim Flaherty.'

McNally told him the little he knew. The little anybody around these parts knew. Blade thanked him and went looking for a horse to rent. Down the street almost on the edge of town, there was a livery stable. It was run by a sawed-off, old, stove-in cowboy named simply Deuce. There Blade found the bay and knew he didn't want to rent it. He wanted to buy it. When he tried the animal out under saddle, his first opinion was confirmed. So he bought it. It set him back two hundred dollars, but he didn't regret it.

Old Deuce said: 'I could ask three hundred for that horse.'

Blade said: 'Then you should have. I would have paid it.'

Deuce looked disgusted and said: 'It amounts to horse-stealing what you just did to me.'

Blade grinned.

'That's what's making me feel so good,' he said.

He bought a Texas rig from a saddlemaker and all the rest of the horse-gear, choosing what he wanted carefully, enjoying to the full the hour he spent in the shop with the craftsman.

The owner shook him by the hand when he left and said: 'Nice to do business with a man who knows what he wants.'

The following morning, Blade rode out to Big Jim Flaherty's place.

He reached it at noon.

Though it had amounted to something once, it now looked to be a poor place. For no reason at all, the fact surprised him. The land looked poor and the place was poor. The land looked as though it were meant for nothing but goats. The house looked run-down. Either it had belonged to somebody who did not care, or to somebody who had more than he could handle. The house was of adobe and looked as though the wind, rain and sun had done their work on it for a hundred years. It was the home of a struggling Mexican.

The woman who answered the door to his hail was, in fact, Mexican. Either she spoke no English or pretended not to. She was plainly apprehensive of him. She was no longer so very young, but she wasn't so very old either. She was still a beauty and she had about her a natural dignity that Blade at once respected. She seemed to relax a little when she heard his fluent Spanish, and agreed to let him water his horse at the well and to sit in the shade of her porch. Then she went into the house, only to come out a moment later wearing a pair of shoes. She wanted to show him that she was not a barefoot peasant woman. Blade was touched.

'I am employed, señora,' he told her, 'by an old friend of your husband. I take it that Jim Flaherty was your husband.'

She shrugged. What did it matter now? 'I am here to find the man who killed him.'

He half-prepared himself for an emotional outburst, but none came. She frowned, puzzled.

'This friend,' she said, 'how does he call himself?'

Blade said he was not able to reveal that. This friend was a powerful man and he wished his name to be kept out of it. Blade told her that he, Blade, wanted all the information about Flaherty that he could get so that he could discover if anybody had actually planned to kill him.

Such a thing was impossible, she said. Everybody knew that it had been a random killing. The man who had shot her man had been some vaquero on the spree from south of the Border. Men were like children with guns. If a man had a gun, sooner or later he would shoot it. One of the tragedies of life was that her Jim had got in the way of the bullet. Or it was an odd Mexican who did not like gringos? The señor knew how it was. Maybe killing a gringo made this man feel good. Who knows? But nothing could bring her man back to life. Possibly, she would now starve.

No, the señora would not starve, Blade assured her. Jim's powerful friend would give her some money. Blade asked her to trust him. What friends did Jim have in these parts?

Everybody was Jim's friend. Texas men, Mexicans, Rangers, rogues, everybody liked him. If the señor had known him, he would have liked him. She never hoped to find another man like him. He had a big heart. Not much of this world's goods, but a great heart. 'Believe me, señor, you could never know a man as great-hearted as Jim,' she told Blade.

He believed her. Or he believed that she believed what she said was the truth. A man is never a hero to everybody.

Yes, she would give him the names of all the men with whom Jim was most friendly. She would do anything to help, though the señor was wasting his time. Nobody around here would ever dare admit that he had killed Big Jim Flaherty.

Blade sighed. He had the unhappy feeling things would get worse before they got better. The attack in Kansas City had been bad enough, but it had been an omen for something a damn sight worse.

The woman's name was Esmeralda. He thought that a pretty name and said so. The woman flashed strong white teeth in a brilliant smile. It transfigured her. Jim Flaherty had been a lucky man to get her.

'There were no little ones,' she said, 'and sometimes that made Jim pretty sad.' She pronounced the name as Jeeem. It sounded like a good name to have, the way she said it.

She told him the names of Jim's friends and he wrote them down. He gave her twenty-five dollars to keep her going. He told her where he was staying in Laredo. Everybody might as well know. She said he was very kind and if there was anything more he wanted to know . . .

He asked if she would be safe alone on the little ranch out in that desolate place.

'There are two cousins of mine out on the range,' she told him. 'They are good men and they will protect me.'

Blade cast his eye over the arid country and asked: 'Where did Jim ever find grass for his cows?'

She pointed in the direction of the foothills, pastel blues and pinks under the blasting rays of the sun. She used the under edge of her hand to point.

'There are breaks in the hills,' she told him. 'There is grass and a little water. Jim preferred it out here.' A little, tight smile. 'He said that it was better to be able to see a long way and see who was coming.'

'A wise man,' Blade commented, made his farewells and rode out.

He headed for the hills and tried the bay out in bad country. The gelding responded well and showed itself to be as surefooted as a goat. There was little to commend the low hills.

They seemed as arid as the plains below. That is, until he came to a break and there he saw the tops of trees and, looking down, saw the pale flash of silver birch and the reflecting surface of water.

As he turned back towards the plain, far out a small wisp of dust caught his eye. He found his glass and put it on the source of the dust. Even without the dust, the distance would have been too great for him to make out any details. He waited patiently and, after a while, he saw that it was a buggy pulled by two horses. They looked like brisk-footed high-steppers. There were two men in the vehicle, side by side on the seat. He could make out little of them except that they wore dark clothing.

He swept the glass then along the trail, to the Flaherty place. Out in front, Esmeralda was shading her eyes with a hand against the sun, watching the approaching vehicle. In her other hand, she held a short saddlegun. In the absence of her cousins, she was apparently prepared to defend herself.

Blade put the glass back on the buggy. Now he could make out the red stripes on the canvas cover. He held the glass on the man beside the driver. There was something vaguely familiar about him. Blade kept the glass on him. His curiosity was aroused.

When the buggy halted and the dust slowly settled, the two fine horses stood tossing their heads. The man beside the driver got down and walked towards the Mexican woman. He was small and thin, dressed in city clothes. When he stood in front of Esmeralda, he uncovered his head.

Blade smiled to himself. The man was Ransome S. Howard.

Now Blade, a man who thought himself to be beyond surprise, was surprised. Howard and the Mexican woman embraced and kissed. Nothing more, except that they went into the house and the door closed behind them. The driver climbed down from the buggy, watered the horses and gave himself a drink at the well. Then he walked up and down, stopping now and then to stare either out across the plain or into the hills in Blade's direction.

Suddenly, the man turned and hurried back to the buggy and reached something from it.

He's seen me, thought Blade, *he's gone for his glass.*

He quickly turned the bay and sought cover. From the concealment of a sweep of brush, Blade saw the glint of sun on binoculars.

The man inspected the hills for some time. Blade did not stir. The man eventually gave up and hung the glasses around his neck. Blade at once put his own glass on the fellow and saw that it was the grey man who had paid him his retainer in Kansas City.

Blade turned the bay into the hills.

The rifle could not have been more than a hundred yards away when it was fired.

Something hit the horn of the saddle in front of Blade and the force of it staggered the horse.

Blade hit the horse with his quirt and it reacted as fast as a well-trained cowpony, jumping and turning in one move. Blade hit it again, knowing his life depended on it. His eyes searched for good cover, and he silently debated whether to keep going or to get out of the saddle. No cover for a man on foot, not from where that rifleman lay. So he kept going.

He never heard the second shot.

The bay squealed piercingly and went down.

Some odd corner of Blade's mind must have prepared him for the eventuality. The old lesson of knowing how to fall off a horse before you learned how to stay on one. He came out of that saddle feet free of the stirrup-irons and running.

No sooner was he running than he knew there was nowhere to run to. A cold shaft of fear cut through him. He turned and dived back towards the horse. Even as he did so, he saw the animal's rolling, terrified eyes. He saw its nearside foreleg failing it pitifully as it fought to rise. In its terror and pain, it kicked aimlessly, venting its desperate helplessness in a scream like that of a stricken woman.

As Blade hit the ground hard, the Colt's gun was in his hand. He rammed the muzzle against the great head and fired.

With a last convulsive series of kicks, the animal lay still and Blade rolled to ram his own length against the saddle and back. The rifle cracked irritably and the bullets thudded fruitlessly into the body of the dead horse. Blade's face was pressed into the coarse hair of the mane, filling his nostrils with the smell of horse.

'You bastard,' he said with quiet bitterness.

He wondered if Howard and the grey man had heard the shots. No need to wonder, he told himself, they must have done so. Whether they would do anything about them was another matter.

Silence.

Blade lay there, listening. He didn't doubt that the dry-gulcher was now changing his position, so that he could get a better view of his target. Blade decided to fill in the time usefully. Maybe he was a dead duck, but he was determined that there would be another dead duck around there before the sun went down.

He had two empty chambers in the Colt. He always kept an empty chamber under the hammer and he had fired one shot. He loaded the Peacemaker so that all six chambers were in the game. Then he reached over and eased the Winchester carbine from the boot. No shot came, but Blade would take no risk. He slid the Colt away into leather and lay listening.

He was alerted by the soft rattle of loose rocks to the north of him and knew that the man was working his way along the edge of the break. While he was concentrating his hearing in that direction, and also craning his neck so that he might see something, he heard the clink of a metal rifle butt on rock in the opposite direction.

Then he knew just how serious the situation was. There were two men and they had him outflanked.

He began to wonder what sort of things men (and women) would say about him after he was dead. Such thoughts were not his favourite ones.

If I always toted a partner around with me like a sensible man, he thought, *this could never happen. These two sons-of-bitches would never get to back-shoot me.*

Which thought was rather late in the day and he knew it. With grim humour, he told himself he would never work alone again – because very shortly he was going to be dead.

From behind him came a high light whistle which meant, he knew, that the man who had worked his way along the top of the break was now in position. A few seconds passed and the man to the south gave an answering whistle.

Here it comes, Blade thought. *This is where they blow me to ribbons.* He wondered, rather to no purpose under the circumstances, what sort of lovers the two Howard ladies would be. Now, he was certain, he would never know. A pity.

He was now in the sights of both marksmen. If they missed him, they shouldn't be in the drygulching business.

He craned his neck and looked back over his left shoulder.

Now he learned something which he had not noticed before. Which showed that the possibility of death sharpened a man's senses wondrously. Not a dozen feet away from him was a small ledge. Most of the area that surrounded him was malpais, mostly a flat area of rock like a smooth island in a sea of rocks and brush and loose dust. From where he lay, the ledge did not seem more than a foot high at best. But to him it was like an answer to a prayer.

The man to the north fired one shot.

In that instant, Blade jerked back his head and the bullet thudded into the saddle. He lay there for a moment very much aware that death had missed him by no more than an inch.

He rolled twice as the second rifle sounded. He heard a

bullet smack into the dead horse, a second strike rock and whine its way to heaven. He drove himself to his feet, took two hurried paces and hurled himself down. During the time it took him to do this, he was dimly aware that both men fired several shots.

He hit rock with his right shoulder and the landing hurt him like hell. He rolled again, reached the brink of the ledge and fell into a bed of brown dust. His mouth was open at the time, sucking in air. A good deal of dust went into it. He choked and both rifles tried to shoot his head off. Choking or not, he drove his face down into the bed of dust and was thankful for it.

Then the shooting stopped.

His heart sang a little. He reckoned they couldn't see him.

He heard a man yell in a voice pitched high with excitement: 'Get him, get him.'

Boots sounded on rock. Spur chains jingled.

Blade moved instinctively now. Forgotten was the Winchester carbine in his left hand. His right hand slapped down on the holster of the Colt and the heavy weapon came free and smooth into his right hand. The sound of the man running guided him unerringly. There was dust in his eyes and the stuff choked his lungs. The figure of the racing man was no more than a ghost figure. To be sure, Blade gave him two shots, one hard upon the heels of the other.

Blade knew he'd hit. His skill would never fail him at that range. The man was still running when Blade swung the gun on to the other man. Vaguely, he saw just head and shoulders. He drove a shot and the form at once disappeared.

Blade swung back to the other man, moving like an impassioned automaton, nerves screaming, his habitual calm broken in the speed and violence of the action.

The man was down, floundering on the flat surface of the rock, twisting and turning.

Blade tried to wipe the dust from his eyes. Desperately, he wanted to see clearly. Where was the other man?

A sound reached him. Horses. Was the other man escaping? No, these were horses approaching. They were coming up the hillside from the plain. Could this be Howard and the grey man coming to make themselves useful?

Another sound – the clink of a spur. Blade whirled. But he was too late. The roar of the gun was deafening. Something smashed into his head.

He didn't know how long he stood there, holding his head in his hands, feeling as if his skull had disintegrated and its contents scattered over the hillside, but he clearly heard the Colt hit rock as he dropped it. He heard boot-heels scraping on rock and he knew that he was doing his best to walk. He had no idea where to. All he knew was that he had to keep moving for some crazy reason beyond his understanding.

Then he was falling, down, down, down into a deep red pit. After an eternity, he hit bottom. He was trying to say something, but a great cold silence came down over him like a cloak and the words never came.

4

Ransome S. Howard was out of sorts. He always was when his affairs did not go smoothly. What was the use, he asked himself, of having several million dollars if your affairs did not go smoothly? That was what money was for, to buy anything you wanted. And he wanted smoothness. He was angry with himself for permitting such a state of affairs. He was angry with the grey man because it was his job to see that matters went smoothly. He was also out of sorts because he had ridden hard up the hillside and he loathed violent physical exercise. Such activity was for the commoner beings of this world.

He climbed down stiffly from his heaving horse and stared coldly at the man who lay dead with two of Blade's bullets in him. He sniffed in disgust.

The grey man swung down from his mount with an agility that belied his years. He bent forward and looked down at Blade.

'I think Blade's still alive, sir.'

Howard walked over and stared down at Blade as coldly as he had inspected the other man.

'He *looks* dead,' he said. 'But I do not give a fig one way or the other. I certainly think he has outlived his usefulness, whatever he is. He has become nothing more than a target.'

'I think we should maybe do something for him, sir,' said the grey man.

'You think what you please,' said Howard. 'But don't express your thoughts to me. Search him and his saddle. And hurry it up or we shall be caught out in this accursed wilderness after dark.'

Ten minutes later, they rode away. Howard did not look back. The grey man halted his horse before he went down over the ridge and stared at the man on the ground. He frowned, wondering how long Blade's face would stay in his mind or would present itself as a memory in the small hours of the night. He pursed his lips and rode on after his employer, looking straight ahead. As they came down off higher ground, he came alongside Howard and said: 'I think we just made a mistake, sir.'

'When did you ever know me make a mistake?' Howard demanded.

'Never till now,' said the grey man. 'If Blade is alive we shall regret it.'

Howard glared at him.

'He will not know that we found him,' he said.

'Blade will, sir, rest assured,' said the grey man.

Howard twisted his thin mouth into a smile.

'Maybe you should go back and make sure of him,' he said.

The grey man said: 'Not quite my style, sir, if you'll pardon the liberty.'

Blade did not die.

No thanks to the unknown men who had attacked him, no thanks to Ransome S. Howard. Maybe thanks to Esmeralda, the woman who had lived with Big Jim Flaherty, but whom Flaherty had not married because she was a Papist and a Mexican. Or so it was assumed.

Blade reached the Flaherty place around midnight and when he did so he was babbling as a man will who is in a high fever and more than half out of his mind.

The Mexican woman took him in as her kind have taken the broken and the unfortunate as long as man can remember. She dragged him inside her simple house and somehow by brute strength and determination got him into her own bed. Then she worked through the night until in the cold dawn hour she watched the fever that was racking his body break.

'*Pobrecito*,' she said, 'don't worry, you will live. You have a good strong body and the will.'

At dawn, her two cousins came into the house and stared down at him, their wide-brimmed hats in their hands, and one of them laughed in affectionate good-humour – '*Prima*, where do you find such men? And always gringos.'

She smiled.

'Go away, you worthless geldings,' she told them. 'They don't have to be gringos. Just men.'

The other cousin laughed and said: 'This poor fellow is at least safe from your misguided passions while he lies unconscious.'

She drove them away. When they were standing outside in the chill of the morning, they held their ponchos close around them. The woman came out of the house and said: 'Do not forget – one of you must always be near the house. There is danger now this man is here.'

The elder, Enrique, said: 'Esmeralda, you should have abandoned your pride and married Jim. Then the land could have been legally yours.'

'Legally mine!' she exclaimed, scandalised by the possibility that it might not be hers. 'I won't listen to such talk. The land *is* legally mine.'

Enrique, who had had the supremacy of the Anglos dinned into him since childhood, said: 'The old claims are worthless, so stop pinning your hopes on such a thing. The Anglos will never recognise your paper.'

'Jim recognised it,' she retorted. 'He always called it my land. The men who tried to kill the gringo there – they recognised it, or why should they have tried to kill him for it?'

The younger cousin, Pablo, raised his dark eyebrows.

'You mean he has it?'

'It is possible.'

Enrique said: 'We should search him.'

Esmeralda said: 'Time enough for that. He is an honest man.'

Pablo said hotly: 'When was any man honest when it came to a fortune?'

Esmeralda said: 'Cousins, be good. Do as you wish. Did I ever fail you?'

They inspected their feet and agreed that she never had. When they raised their eyes to look at her, they were smiling, their white teeth contrasting with the brown of their skins.

Enrique said: 'We will both stay, *muchaca.* Two guns are better than one and there must be no danger for you.'

'There is much to do about the place,' said Pablo. 'We shall work and watch.'

She watched them walk away, two men made hard by a hard land, their spurs crashing on their sandalled feet.

One day, she thought, *I shall buy them fine boots such as the Yanquis wear.*

She went back into the house and saw that the gringo's eyes were open and were watching her. She sat on the wooden frame of the string bed and took his hand in hers.

'*Muy bien,*' she said, 'so you have decided that it is better to live.'

'How did I get here?' he asked in a whisper.

'You walked.'

'Impossible.'

She laughed and told him how she had sat through the night with him. Now she would feed him and make him strong again. Within a week, he would be on his feet.

He lay there frowning, his prematurely grey hair lost in the bandages she had swathed it in. Trying to remember, he found himself facing a blank. There was something . . . a small thread and he clung to it. A small moment from the immediate past – a horse. Blade heard the scream of the animal. He tried to sit up and the woman's strong hands forced him back on the bed.

'You must be still,' she said. 'You will bleed again.'

'My horse,' he said in English. 'The bastards shot my horse.'

For a moment, she thought he would weep. Instead of which, his eyes darkened with rage.

'Don't fret,' she said. 'You will find them again. Or they will find you.'

He stared at her.

'I heard Howard's voice,' he said.

She looked scared now and turned instinctively as though she expected to find the man in the room with them.

'I heard it then,' he said, 'when my horse died.'

'Sleep,' she said. 'All will come right when you are strong again.'

He asked for his gun and seemed suspicious of her for taking it from him. But his suspicions were allayed when she brought it to him without a word and laid the big weapon by his side.

'Sleep without fear,' she said. 'My two cousins are standing guard, and they are good men.'

He grinned and said: 'You mean they're real? I thought you dreamed them up to warn me off.'

His eyes closed and at once he slept. She sat watching him for a while and once she touched the grey stubble on his chin with a gentle hand. She said to herself: 'I think perhaps this one is *mucho hombre*. Like Jim, but with more iron in his soul. Jim did not have too much iron.'

'Why do you think, dear step-mother,' June Howard asked, 'that my father brought you and I to this God-forsaken place?'

'For a number of reasons, dear step-daughter,' said Mrs Howard, looking as tranquil as a saint. 'Your father likes to keep his possessions in sight in case other men should take them. Another reason is that he does not trust us.'

'But why is *he* here?' June said.

Mrs Howard suggested: 'As you are closest to him, you should ask him.'

June changed tack: 'Wouldn't it be more sensible, Narcissa, for us to be allies instead of enemies?'

The older woman said: 'We are most certainly not enemies, June. But I see no reason why we should be allies.'

'Do you ever lose your temper?'

Narcissa smiled.

'I have done, but I've shown it only once.'

'Why did you marry my father?'

Narcissa replied: 'You would like me to say "for his money". So I'll say: "For his money". Does that satisfy you?'

The door opened and they both turned from the hotel window to see Howard standing in the open doorway.

'Good morning, my dears,' he said. He looked pale and his face was drawn. They knew that he had arrived back in town late, covered with dust and looking unusually anxious. They both knew that something was wrong.

'Ransome,' Narcissa said, 'has something happened?'

Rather nastily, he replied. 'Something frequently happens, my dear. This time it is a small matter with which you need not worry your pretty heads.' He smiled gruesomely at the pair of them. Neither responded. 'Last night, we discovered that the man I hired in Kansas City had been killed.'

June drew her breath in sharply.

'You can't mean Joe Blade.' She seemed unable to get her voice above a whisper.

He turned his cold eyes on her.

'That is precisely what I mean, my dear,' he said. He did not take his eyes from her face. 'You look distressed. You cannot possibly mean that this man meant anything to you. You didn't know him.'

June was annoyed with herself for having shown her feelings. She recovered herself quickly, but Narcissa did not miss her reaction to the news of Blade's death. She steeled herself to remain calm, already trying to deny to herself that Blade had made any impression on her, Narcissa.

'June spoke to him once, Ransome,' she explained. 'It's a shock to hear of the violent death of someone one has met even only once.'

June gave her a look of gratitude.

Narcissa asked: 'How did he die?'

Howard said: 'As one would expect of that kind, he was shot.'

'What kind?' June asked in a voice that shook a little.

Howard looked a little surprised by the question – 'Why, he was a gunman, of course.'

June then asked a question that startled him – 'Why should you hire a gunman, father?'

The question caught him unawares and, for a moment, he did not know what to reply.

'In this instant,' he said finally, 'I was using him as an investigator. He had some skill and experience, not to say fame, in that direction.'

June asked: 'What are we doing down here in this place, father?'

'By that, I presume you mean what am *I* doing,' he said. 'The answer to that is that I have some land interests here.'

She said: 'There doesn't seem to be any land worth having.'

He said shortly: 'That depends on the amount and its relative position.' With which words, he put his hands behind his back and walked from the room, looking, with his forward thrusting head and hunched shoulders, very much like a bird of prey.

The two women exchanged glances.

'It's hard to believe,' Narcissa said.

Unreasonably, June said: 'He didn't seem the kind of man who could be killed.'

For a moment, the two were drawn closer together. Narcissa looked out of the window on to the street. The local Mexicans seemed to move no faster than the sluggish warm breeze. There was an air of *mañana* over the whole scene. There was a sudden eddy of movement among the passers-by. Ransome S. Howard had lunged out of the hotel and was walking down the street. In his dark suit and purposeful air, he looked entirely out of place.

'I'm going to ask Chard about it,' Narcissa said. 'He was with your father last night.'

June said: 'He'll tell you nothing. He's very much father's man.'

Narcissa turned to the door – 'He is also his own. I have a feeling about Chard. He doesn't say much and he's been with Ransome since the early days, but there are times when I think that, in some ways, he is a stronger character than your father.'

'That sounds crazy,' June said. 'He does everything father tells him. He's little more than an intelligent slave. Why, I think he'd kill for father if he was asked.'

Narcissa stopped at the door and said: 'And probably has, but that doesn't alter my feelings. I think, for example, that he has a strong sympathy for you, June.'

June was surprised – 'Me? Why he scarcely speaks to me and then only in disapproval.'

'Come with me to see him,' Narcissa said. 'If you're with me maybe I shall get what we want.'

As she went out of the room, she felt her step-daughter's hand on her arm. She turned to find a strange look on June's face. It seemed odd, but on anybody else she would have interpreted the look as one of respect.

June said: 'I think we *are* allies, Narcissa.'

The older woman patted the younger's hand and said: 'Maybe we should be at that, if we had any sense.'

They went to the room which Howard used as an office and there they found the grey man, Chard, sitting at his desk. It was the position they were used to seeing him in, crouched over paper, pen scratching away. At the sound of their entrance, he looked up, appearing faintly surprised to see them, but at once came to his feet.

'Good morning, ladies.'

'Good morning, Mr Chard,' Narcissa said. She hesitated for no more than a second before she shot at him: 'Is it true that Joe Blade is dead?'

The grey man was startled. He looked around hastily, as if searching for somebody to save him from these two women.

'Saints alive, Miss Narcissa,' he said, 'that is some question, if I may say so.'

'That does not prevent it from being answerable, Mr Chard,' she said.

It was his turn to hesitate and he did so for no more than a second. They were not to know that the man Blade had been on Chard's conscience ever since he had looked down on his bloody face on the hill. Abruptly, he seemed to make up his mind.

'When I last saw him,' he said, 'he was hurt. It would have been the opinion of most men that he would die.'

Narcissa cried: 'And you did nothing to help him?'

'Let us say, ma'am, that it was beyond my power to help him.'

'You may say it as much as you wish, sir,' June cut in. 'But was it so? What possible circumtances could a man find himself in that would prevent him from giving Christian aid to a wounded man?'

Chard took on a hunted look, fighting to retain his usual calm image.

'I would say, Miss June,' he said, 'that Blade is not a man who dies easily. I would wager that he had survived.'

Narcissa said: 'Are you able to check whether he lived or died, Mr Chard?'

He looked distressed. He looked at June as though she might

rescue him from this situation, but the expression on her face told him that he could expect no help there.

'I am *able*, Miss Narcissa,' he said. 'But I am sure that Mr Howard would not approve.'

'We did not think for one moment that he would,' said June. 'We are also sure, Mr Chard, that you are capable of independent action on your own initiative.'

'I am indeed,' he said, but there was doubt in his voice. Now he became so agitated that he could not remain still. He clenched and unclenched his hands while the two women watched him in amazement. They had never seen this man anything but calm and granite-faced. 'Oh, ladies, you put me in a dreadful situation, an impossible position. You appeal to my better nature, but I have never committed a disloyal act in my life.'

'Maybe it's time, Mr Chard, that you were loyal to yourself,' said Narcissa.

He turned and looked at her, wide-eyed.

'This is uncanny, ma'am,' he said. 'I had only just uttered those very words to myself.'

'And what did you answer yourself?'

'I have *not* answered myself.'

'Where has my husband gone?'

'I don't know, ma'am. But he will be gone until the evening meal or later.'

'Would that give you time to find out about Mr Blade?'

The hunted look came back again. 'If he's still alive, he would not be where I saw him.'

'Then go there. If he's gone, we'll know he's alive.'

'The men who killed him may have returned and removed the body.'

June said: 'We *must* know, Mr Chard.'

As they watched him, they saw a look of almost desperate determination come over his face. He slammed one fist into a palm and cried: 'By God, ladies, I *shall* go.'

But when Narcissa suggested that they go with him he looked alarmed – 'Most certainly not, ma'am,' he said. 'It is far too dangerous for you. Now, I need a fast horse. With luck I shall be back late this afternoon.'

June went to him and laid a hand on his arm.

'Mr Chard,' she said, giving him the full devastating benefit of her beautiful eyes, 'you have the undying gratitude of two very helpless women.'

When he smiled, they both realised that they had never seen him smile before.

'Ladies,' he said with a little bow, 'it is an honour and a privilege. Only, I beg of you, let this stay a secret between the three of us.'

5

Chard rode a horse in the same manner that he did all things – solidly and without show. He chose a horse at the livery very much like himself – a no-nonsense work-horse that would get him there and back without tantrums and with no wild rushes. An animal that would do what was demanded of it and would not panic at anything unusual.

Being a man who left as little as possible to chance, Chard had armed himself well, strapping a Colt Peacemaker to his waist and putting a small pocket Remington in his jacket. Thus equipped, and keeping a sharp eye open on the country, he rode to the spot where he and Howard had left what they thought to be the dying Blade.

Chard had to admit to himself that he had known no greater relief in his life than when the two Howard ladies had forced him to make the moral decision to return to the spot. For, though he scarcely admitted the fact to himself, the thought of leaving a man to die had weighed heavily on his conscience. They had revealed to him just how much he had deadened his feelings since he had been in the employ of Ransome S. Howard. Now he faced the fact that he had done too many things for his employer which any decent man would have been ashamed of.

But he did not expect to find Blade there, and he was right. He did, however, find the remains of the dead horse, though the varmints had been at it and had largely consumed it. From the spot, he looked out over the plain and there right beneath him was the house of Big Jim Flaherty.

Chard gazed at it and scratched his chin.

There was nowhere else for Blade to go, he told himself. *If he went anywhere, it had to be there.*

Chard hesitated. It was the Mexican woman who made him pause. She would inform Howard that he had been here. And Chard feared Howard.

Just the same, and greatly to his credit, Chard determined that, if he had come thus far to ease his conscience, he must carry the project to its logical conclusion.

He therefore headed his horse down the hillside in the direction of the house. Down on the flat, he was startled to be challenged by a grim-faced Mexican with an old single-shot Remington rifle in his hands. This bandit-like figure seemed to appear from out of the ground itself.

In not very good English, the man said: 'Who are you and what do you want here?'

He knew the relationship between Howard and the woman, so this greeting surprised him. Then the awful thought hit him that the men who opposed Mr Howard, possibly the men who had shot Blade, might now be in possession of the house. The thought was a scary one and he was greatly puzzled what to do and say.

However, he made up his mind to tell the truth and leave the rest to providence.

'My name is Chard,' he said. 'I am the man of business to Mr Ransome S. Howard. I wish to speak to Señorita Santiago.'

The man shrugged and sneered a little.

'Just like that,' he said. 'You think you can ride up here and speak to the señorita as if she were a nobody.'

'If you tell her that I come from Mr Howard, I am sure—'

The man jerked his head towards the house – 'Go to the house. She is there. She knows you have come. We have been watching you for a long time.'

Chard rode on towards the house, feeling considerably

annoyed. He felt that damned Mexican in his leather clothes with his old gun had been laughing at him.

He dismounted at the hitch-rail and tied his horse. The door of the house was ajar. The inside looked very cool and dark. He wondered whether he should go in.

'Señorita,' he called.

She appeared in the doorway. 'Yes? So you finally decided to come here.'

'I have come from Mr Howard and would like to speak to you.'

Her English was so good, it took him by surprise. From her dress and what he had heard of her, he expected a peasant. This was the first time he had spoken to her. It was also the first time he had seen her at close quarters. She was, he could see, a remarkably handsome woman. Those dark dramatic Mexican eyes quite set him back.

'You are free to speak,' she said.

'May I come inside?'

'It is not proper that you should come inside out of the sight of the man there,' she replied primly. The eyes were brightly intelligent and had an ironic touch of humour in them. Her body was that of a strong animal. A mountain cat. Back in Kansas City, he had heard shocking tales about Mexican women. Now, in a moment of wildness that was strange to him, he hoped it was true. Maybe it was the terrible heat of this place that was affecting him. For the first time for many years, he felt that he wanted to live.

He had to remind himself that he had come here to find Blade. He decided on the spur of the moment to come out into the open about his mission.

'I am looking for the man called Blade,' he said.

The expression on her face did not change, but he saw the sudden alarm in her expressive eyes. He knew then that either the man was here or she knew where he was.

'What makes you think he is here?' she demanded.

'I do not necessarily think he's here, ma'am,' Chard said. 'But he lay injured up on the hill there. This is the nearest place where he could possibly find help.'

She said: 'Why this sudden interest in this man? You saw him when he lay wounded yesterday.'

'That's true,' he said. 'Yesterday I was unable to help. Today I wish to make amends.'

Said out loud, he thought that sounded pretty weak.

For a moment, she stared at him as though she did not know what to do.

'He is unconscious,' she told him. 'Maybe he is dying, I do not know. But he is a very sick man. Ransome Howard sent you?'

This was a day for truth, he decided. He shook his head. 'No, no. I came on my own account.'

She opened the door wide and said: 'Come inside.'

He uncovered his head and followed her into the house. The house was dim and cool after the heat and bright sunlight of the world outside. It took the grey man a full minute to adjust his eyes so that he could make out objects. The house seemed to be L-shaped, consisting of a single, big room with a small kitchen attached to one end of it. In the middle of the room was a rope bed with a man lying on it. He was very still and his eyes were shut. Chard went near and looked down at him. It was not easy at first to recognise Blade in this man with unshaven sunken cheeks, deep-set eyes. He was pale enough to be near death.

Chard asked: 'How did he reach here?'

'He crawled,' the woman told him. 'What is Mr Howard's interest in this man?'

Experiencing an unusual feeling of malice towards his employer, Chard said: 'None now. He is through with him.'

Chard nearly took leave of his skin a moment later, when he saw the man on the bed open his eyes. The blanket was thrown back. Chard saw that there was a gun in Blade's hand. It pointed at the grey man's heart.

'I'm not through with Howard,' Blade said, loud and clear.

Chard was amazed at the strength of the voice. This man was hurt, all right, but he didn't look too near death right now.

Chard wanted to say something, to clear himself with this man. Guilt gibed at him like a spur. He went to say something, but he felt that words would be totally inadequate and stayed silent.

Blade was saying: 'We have a contract, remember? And you owe me one thousand dollars. You hired me for a target without telling me. So I was suckered. But Howard pays or I take it out on his hide. Maybe you think changing a fee is unethical, Mr Chard, but anybody in my profession charges a higher fee when his life is at risk.'

Chard said: 'I can assure you, Mr Blade, that we had no idea if you were at risk.' Then he realised he couldn't speak for his employer. How could Chard know that Howard had not been as smart as usual? Too damn smart for his own or anybody else's good.

'But the opposition tried to kill me just the same,' Blade said. 'Both here and in Kansas City.'

'We could not fortell that,' Chard said weakly.

'Like hell you couldn't,' said Blade. 'What were they looking for? Something small? Something that could be stitched into the seam of a coat or into the leather of a saddle?'

Suddenly Chard was a very worried man. He was out of his depth. He stole a look at the woman. Esmeralda Santiago's eyes were on him and he could see the smouldering anger in them.

By God, he thought, *this damned woman scares me. Howard has bitten off more than he can chew with her.*

'So,' she said, 'Howard has lied to me. He comes and kisses me like a long-lost brother because I am the woman of his beloved old friend, Jim Flaherty. It is the kiss of Judas that he gives me.'

Blade was temporarily forgotten. He lay there, taking it all in, suddenly realising that here was the chance of finding the key.

'Miss Santiago,' Chard stammered, wishing more than ever that he had not come, knowing that he was on the brink of betraying his employer. 'I am sure that I can explain.'

'Howard told me that he held the paper,' she said. 'He searched Blade for it. You ripped up his saddle to look for it. When his hotel room was searched, those men were looking for it. My God, what have you done to me between you? Howard and his enemies are both after that paper.'

'Believe me,' Chard said, 'Mr Howard will see that you do not lose by the transaction.'

He winced visibly as her rage exploded.

'I do not intend to lose by any transaction,' she cried. 'Though I would lose if I had any transaction with your accursed master. I intend to hold on to my land. It has been in my family since two hundred years and I do not intend to have it taken from me by the Yanquis like every other person of my race.'

Chard said: 'I am sure that, for old time's sake, Mr Howard has your interest at heart.' He told himself that it sounded like a lie as he said it.

The woman cried: 'Ha!' in disgust. Her gesticulation with her right hand was magnificently Mexican. 'There is this wonderful friendship with my man, Jim. But was it so wonderful? Jim sells Howard his share of the business for no more than a few dollars. Where is the friendship in that? Heh? Jim believes that the business is bankrupt and Howard is laughing. My Jim was gullible. Your Howard is a rogue. He comes here and he kisses me and tells me that he will look after the woman of his old friend. He takes Jim's fortune, now he wants my land because he thinks he can get his hands on the Spanish paper. He tells me it is worthless in a Yanqui court. Then why does he want it so much? I see you stand there with a guilty look on your face. You know I speak the truth.'

The impassioned speech seemed to exhaust Esmeralda. She sat down and looked from one man to the other. It was only now that she and Chard remembered the wounded man.

Blade chuckled.

'I'd say that was telling you, Chard,' he said. 'So I've nearly been killed twice for a piece of Spanish paper. Go back and tell Howard I'm still alive and still need paying.'

'I'm sorry this happened, Blade,' Chard said. 'All of it – this business over the land, you being hurt. It is all so unnecessary.'

'You're part of it,' Blade told him. Chard looked at the floor, glanced at Esmeralda and found her furious gaze too much to withstand, and looked away again. He tried to dismiss the subject with a sweep of his hand.

'The Howard ladies are concerned for you,' he said. 'It was they who persuaded me to come here.'

'God bless the ladies,' declared Blade, smiling like an angel.

Chard prepared to depart. He looked at Blade hesitatingly, looked as though he would say something more and thought better of it. He reached the doorway and turned back to say: 'The ladies will be greatly relieved to know that you are alive. As I am.' Then he was gone out into the bright sunlight. The woman followed him. When he had untied his horse and stepped into the saddle, he stayed still for a moment looking down at her. He wished that he had started off better with her and under better circumstances.

By God, he thought, *if I were Ransome Howard I would not waste my time trying to take the land away from this woman. I would take her.* With which daring thought, he reined the horse around, lifted his hand in farewell to her, telling her that he hoped they would meet again under more pleasant circumstances, and rode away.

She went back into the house, thoughtful and worried.

Blade was watching her.

'So,' she said, 'now you know.'

'Now I know,' he said. 'I also know something more and which is of the greatest importance.' He could see the question on her face. 'Your family name is Santiago. So was my mother's. You are the daughter of my mother's second cousin. We are, in short, kissing kin.'

'It is not possible.'

'Certainly it's possible. My name is José Santiago Espada. Joe Blade.'

Her face lit up then in a great smile – 'But of course.'

'Now,' he went on, 'being a kinsman of yours solves a whole lot of problems for me.'

'Such as?'

'It makes it possible for me to help you. Nobody refuses help from a member of the family. I would like to repay my debt to you. I owe you my life.'

She sat on the bed and took his hand. 'It is good to have a man in the house again. It has been lonely without Jim.'

'Let's talk business, Esmeralda,' Blade said. 'Do you have a map? Can you show me where your Spanish grant runs? Can you prove that this piece of paper is of any worth at all?'

This angered her a little and she snatched her hand from his – 'What do I have to prove? It is a grant from the King of Spain himself. It is the oldest claim to land in all New Spain. This land belonged to my family before there was ever a place called Texas.'

'I've seen the courts play hell with these Spanish grants,' he said. 'It would be smart to also have a modern American claim to the land. Mind you, you have a certain amount of protection under the law of naked possession.'

She raised her eyebrows – 'Naked possession. It sounds indecent.'

'It means that there is general knowledge that you have

occupied the land for a long time. Every one knows you have lived here, so you must own the land.'

'Joe,' she said, 'there must be several people who place value on my Spanish paper. Else why should they be willing to kill for it?'

'Have you ever stopped to think they could be wrong?' Blade asked. 'My advice is get a modern claim made out. Let me see the map and I will tell you if it can be done.'

She found the map and propped him up in bed so they could study it together. She sat on the bed beside him with an arm around him to keep him upright. He knew that he was getting stronger when he found the woman more attractive than the map.

'How can I concentrate on the map,' he said, 'when a beautiful woman has an arm around me?'

She laughed – 'That is my intention. I am without principle, as you shall find, amigo. I am the magnet that will draw you back to health and strength.'

He kissed her. It was a long kiss, and the enjoyment of it seemed to increase by the second until the pleasure of it seemed to tingle in his very toes. When she pulled her mouth back from his, she whispered: 'You look very pale. I think that you should lie down.'

'Passed unanimously,' he said.

She lay him down tenderly and suddenly she was beside him.

'We will study the map a little later,' she said softly. Her eyes were moist.

'There are times,' he said, 'when a man is thankful to be shot.'

She laughed and offered him her mouth again.

'These Howard women,' she said, 'are they so very beautiful?'

'They are in Laredo and you are here. Therefore you must be the more beautiful.'

'I don't think that is any answer at all.'

'Is this any kind of answer?' He whipped the blanket back and whisked it over her. They came together and held each other. He could feel the warmth of her strong body seep into his bones. He felt remarkably strong for a man who had crawled from the hills with his head split by a bullet.

After they had made love and lay contentedly in each other's arms, Blade came to thinking about the land and the woman. What could there be on this land so valuable that men would kill for it?

He smiled to himself. What easier than to ask Esmeralda?

'Esmeralda,' he said, 'what makes this land so valuable?'

She rolled over and lay with her fine breasts resting on his chest. She smiled and said: 'You would never guess in a thousand years, it is so simple.'

'Gold?'

'No.'

'It has to be some kind of metal.'

'It does?' she said, still smiling. 'When you are strong enough to sit a horse, I will take you and show you something.'

'Under this treatment – two days. You're strong medicine, woman.'

That pleased her and she kissed him – 'You are good for me, Blade. No man was ever better. No, I shall not let you out of this bed for a week. We shall continue the treatment at regular intervals, as all good doctors recommend.'

'You're greedy,' he accused.

'No,' she said, 'just hungry.'

6

Chard looked at the sky and worried.

He wanted to be back in Laredo by nightfall. His visit to the Santiago place had taken longer than he had anticipated. Not only could there be danger after dark, but he also wanted to be back in his office before his employer returned.

He was right to be worried, for they caught him in open country in the last of the daylight.

He heard them behind him on the Laredo road, coming fast, three of them. They rode good horses and were hitting a killing pace. They meant to catch him before he could near town and the eyes of men could witness what was happening.

In the past, he had often wondered what would happen under such circumstances. There was little he could do until they came up with him, except to run for it. A man could scarcely open fire on what could prove to be three innocuous horseback riders on a lonely trail. He quickened his pace, but by now his horse was tired from the long ride. He debated whether to pull off the trail, but hesitated to make a fool of himself in the eyes of possibly innocent strangers.

He decided that he would ride on as if he did not have a care in the world, but when they came near him, his sense of danger became too much for him and he did not care whether he looked a fool or not. After all, he argued with himself, the country was running with cut-throats and thieves and a man had every right to play it safe. He even went so far as to draw his Peacemaker as he reined in his horse and sat beside the trail with the big gun laid ready on his thigh for use.

They pulled in their horses and the animals stood blowing noisily while their riders sat there staring at Chard.

He lifted the gun and shouted: 'Ride on, gentlemen.'

'For God's sake,' said one of them, feigning enormous astonishment, 'what's this?' He was a big fellow with a sweep of black beard. His small sharp eyes flashed under thick beetling brows. He kept his hands in view on the saddlehorn. 'Are you a thief or somethin'?'

Chard said coldly: 'I would hardly tell you ride on if I were a thief, my good man.'

'Your good man!' shouted a small wiry fellow with a lot of Adam's apple and a ginger moustache. 'You're talkin' to three Texas Rangers, sir. Three officers of the good ole state of Texas. It don't seem right for you to go around brandishing firearms under the noses of honest lawmen. Put the gun up, like a sensible fellow.'

With this, they began to edge their horses nearer to him, one by one, an inch at a time.

'Keep back,' cried Chard, alarm rising in him. 'I'll drop the next man to move towards me.'

The black-bearded fellow said: 'Threatening officers of the law. We could take you in for that.'

Chard said: 'That won't prevent one of you lying dead on the trail there. I warn you, I can use this weapon.'

The horses were at once held on tight reins and the ginger moustache said: 'I reckon he means it, boys.'

'You'd best believe I do,' said Chard.

'Just the same,' said the third man, a sober-looking fellow who might have been a preacher in better days, 'we have to search you, neighbour. There's been a heap of illegal branding hereabouts and maybe you be carryin' a runnin'-iron in your boot-top.'

'Nobody's searching anybody,' said Chard firmly. 'I'll give you a count of three and then I fire.'

They looked, nonplussed, scandalised, as if they had never before met a situation like this.

Then the black-bearded man said: 'It's a Mexican standoff, pards. I'm for goin' back.'

Chard thought: *They must think I was born yesterday.*

Black-beard turned his horse and started at a walk back down the trail. After he had gone no more than a dozen yards, he halted and turned back to face Chard again.

Howard's man-of-business experienced a flutter of fright. He knew that he was outflanked. The slight scare put more iron into him. Chard was the kind of man whose courage grows out of obstinacy. He thrust out his chin doggedly and made up his mind he wasn't going to be beaten by this hangdog trio.

'All of you move,' he shouted. 'Go ahead now. Both of you follow your friend.'

The preacher-like man said: 'I have no wish to go back thataway, sir. I shall continue on to Laredo.'

He started to move on.

'No,' cried Chard, 'turn around.'

The man ignored Chard's order and touched his horse with the spurs, saying: 'My God, sir, you wouldn't shoot a man for going home.'

The fellow now had Chard's attention and no sooner did his eyes start to follow this one than the fellow with the black beard produced his revolver from its scabbard at his side and let fly.

The only thing that saved Chard's life in that moment was the movement on the part of the marksman's horse. The shot came close enough to scare the daylights out of him. Chard's horse jumped at the closeness of the bullet and thus ruined Chard's aim or he would certainly have killed the man who was trying to sneak down the trail towards Laredo. This man yelled in shocked surprise at being shot at and, indeed, was so enraged that he drew his own gun and blazed away at poor Chard as if he had no other wish than to stretch his lifeless form beside the Laredo trail.

Suddenly, every scrap of fear Chard may have experienced now left him. His dander was up. He held his horse in tight and, knowing that he wanted the way to town clear, he fired a second time at the preacher-like man. This shot was more fortunate than the first and took the target under the left armpit, knocking the man from the saddle. He landed in the dust with a great hullaballoo, bawling that he was killed plumb dead.

The fellow with the Adam's apple and ginger moustache seemed undecided whether to attempt Chard's murder or to run for his life. Chard decided the matter for him, by first sending a shot in his direction and then putting spurs to his horse.

The stout animal jumped forward willingly enough, reached the trail and narrowly missed the horse of the man who was desperately trying to escape any further risk. The fellow with the black beard gave a great bellow and came charging forward, firing as he came.

Chard, not seeing any profit in exchanging shots with the enemy and, knowing that his best chance of a healthy future lay in reaching Laredo, turned his horse down the road and sent it racing south.

The man with the black beard followed him for about two miles, yelling and shooting to no purpose. He did gain a little on the grey man, but the bay kept a good pace while Chard now and then sent a shot back over his shoulder to remind his pursuer that he was armed. Finally, black beard thought better of it and turned back, bellowing insults and obscenities after the fleeing man.

Chard rode on, scarcely lessening his pace until he reached the outskirts of Laredo. Although he was feeling somewhat ruffled by his experience, at the same time he felt wonderfully invigorated.

I never knew myself for a man of action, he told himself. *Maybe I'm mistaken in my role in life after all.* He had not done so badly back there on the trail. They were three dangerous ruffians and he had seen them off, even left one of them wounded in the dust. A fellow of Blade's calibre could not have done much better.

Now, he asked himself, were they simply three road-agents after his cash, or were they after him, Chard, in particular? Were they connected in some way with the men who had left Blade for dead? Were they in cahoots with the men who had searched Blade's room in Kansas City? That was a poser for sure. He rode into Laredo and pretty soon he could see the masts of the ships at the quay. Hastily, he found the livery, handed over the horse and hurried to the hotel on foot.

As he entered the room that was used by himself and Howard as an office, his heart went cold. Ransome S. Howard turned from the window to face him.

'Good evening, sir,' Chard said, forcing himself consciously back into his part of the humble employee.

'I see you have been riding,' Howard said. He couldn't see Howard's face. The little man had his back to the window.

Chard went and stood by his desk. That was his proper place. He always felt better by a desk.

'That is correct, sir.'

'I understood that you would remain here and work on my papers,' Howard said.

Chard lifted up his head and looked him in the face.

'There is a note of criticism in your voice, sir,' he said. 'It is misplaced, I assure you.'

Howard suddenly snapped into anger. 'You may assure me of what you like. But that does not alter the fact that you have disobeyed my orders. Where did you go?'

'To the Santiago place.'

'What?' Howard's anger became pure rage.

'The man Blade is alive, sir.'

Howard was shaking. Though Chard still could not see his face clearly, he thought that he had turned pale.

'He knows we left him to die,' Chard went on. 'Both he and Miss Santiago seemed to be aware that you want possession of the Spanish script.' Howard did not say a word. 'On the way back here, I was attacked by three armed men. I think they intended to kill me.'

Icily, Howard said: 'Which apparently they did not succeed in doing.'

'No. I shot one of them and managed to escape.'

'My, my, Chard, we have had an eventful day. You have, however, failed to inform me of one fact.'

'What is that?'

'Why you went at all.'

Chard said: 'To see if Blade was still alive.'

'Don't tell me you have developed a conscience, Chard.' Howard's tone stung the man.

Chard almost snapped back: 'I was never without one.'

Howard stayed silent, hunched up like a bird on its perch. Chard would like to have been able to read his mind. Howard said softly: 'Possibly you now have further thoughts on where the Spanish paper is?'

Chard was of the opinion that Esmeralda Santiago had it, but he experienced a sudden reluctance to tell Howard that. Chard said: 'The opposition think Blade has it. They think you hired him to protect it. That is his reputation: safer than a bank. One reason why I do not think that you can afford to have him dead. I do not know where it is.'

'I think I shall move without it,' Howard said. 'How would you advise me?'

Chard was in a hard place. From habit, he wanted Howard to have the land. For too long he had identified the man's wishes with his own. Yet he had no wish for Esmeralda Santiago to lose it. He was on a slippery slope. The women had got to him and softened him, the two Howard women and the Mexican woman. He did not dislike the situation in which he found himself. To his pleasure, he found that he quite enjoyed it. He hadn't felt this way since he was a kid.

'How can you move without it?' he asked. 'You have stated that it is a legally sound paper and that no claimant to the land would feel safe without it.'

'Damn you, Chard,' Howard cried, 'don't you go quoting me to me. I know perfectly well what I said. But I don't know what's on that paper. I never saw it in my life.' He gave an exclamation of disgust and stomped out of the room.

Almost immediately, the door opened again and June Howard stood in front of Chard, waiting for him to speak.

'He's alive, Miss June,' he said and watched her face come alive.

'That's wonderful,' she said. 'I must tell Narcissa. Thank you, Mr Chard.'

'My pleasure,' he said and felt strangely virtuous. Then she was gone, leaving him alone with the turmoil of his thoughts. He knew that he had lied to Howard about his conscience. He had not retained it all these years. It was only now that he was aware that he'd lost it. It had taken these women to bring him back to it.

So I have a conscience now, he thought. *That is going to be something to contend with. I wonder if life is going to be at all bearable from here on.*

He sat at his desk and pulled a ledger before him. But he made no attempt to work. He kept seeing Esmeralda Santiago's face and he knew that he envied Blade out there, wounded in her bed.

7

Esmeralda was excited and she was not one to hide her emotions. She became animated. Suddenly, she was fully alive. They had decided that Blade was strong enough for a fairly long ride, a fact he'd been aware of for some days.

Enrique found him a small Spanish horse and saddle. Blade constantly found the two Mexicans staring at him possessively now they knew he was a kinsman. They smiled a lot when they addressed him as *primo.* This morning they saddled a pretty little strawberry roan mare for Esmeralda. Enrique announced: 'I shall ride with you so that you may be protected against the bandidos. Pablo will stay here and guard the house.'

They rode straight into the hills, Esmeralda sitting a hand-carved side-saddle and looking every inch a Mexican lady in her black sombrero and black riding habit.

They rode about four miles into the hills, taking an ancient trail that must have been used in the days of the Spaniards. The land was arid and desolate. One of those countries, as Blade could see, that produced nothing but mesquite and rocks. Here there was even precious little mesquite except where there was poor water in a few hollows.

As for Blade, but for a slight headache, he felt like a new man. Esmeralda had removed the bandage from his head and there was now along the side of his forehead nothing more than a puckered scar to show where he had been creased by the bullet. Already being in the saddle made him feel better. A day or two on the back of a horse, he told himself, and he would be as good as ever.

On high ground from which they could see miles out over the country, Esmeralda halted and pointed: 'Look.'

Blade squinted against the sun and tried to pierce the heat haze below.

'What am I supposed to see?' he demanded.

'There, there.'

He thought he could make out a thin ribbon that glistened across the land. It cut straight into the hills from the Rio Grande.

'A canal?' he asked.

'*Acequia madre*,' she replied. 'That is the mother ditch. Now, come, I will show you something more.'

She walked her horse on and the two men followed. They had not gone far when she halted again and pointed. 'That is where the children of the mother go.'

He could scarcely believe his eyes. Below them was a valley, maybe three miles across and almost twenty long. Here were many ribbons of water cutting like pale arteries through the body of the land. Between them the land was so green that it was hard for the mind to accept it.

'I can't believe it,' Blade said. It didn't seem possible, not down here in this corner of Texas so close to the Mexican Border. It was like coming on Eden in the desert.

'Now,' she said, 'you can see why the men want my land.'

So it was as simple as that. The land could be irrigated. Suddenly the Santiago acres were priceless.

'You mean you're going to bring water to your land and make a fortune?' he said.

'Down there is the evidence that it can be done,' she said. 'This valley belongs to Ransome Howard. He knows very well now what it is worth. And he wants more. The Howards of this world always want more. He has had experts look at my soil and he knows my land is even better than his.'

'And there are other men who want your land?'

'That is so, but I do not know who,' she replied. 'And they

want my Spanish paper enough to kill for it, so it must be valuable.'

He asked: 'You plan to irrigate your land as Howard has done here?'

She made a wholly Mexican gesture and screwed up her face in disgust. 'That will take money and that is something I do not have. Always my family has been poor. I have a few cattle and much land. The pressure on me to sell some land is very great, but I want to keep it all together. Howard has offered me money, he has offered to have the ditches dug for me. But at a price. A half-share in the land. Joe, I think that is why Jim died.'

Blade looked at her. 'Are you saying Howard killed him?'

'It is possible. We know they once were partners. We know Howard swindled him. Maybe he killed Jim when Jim agreed with me that I should not part with my land. What was good for me, Jim always said, was good for him too.'

Blade said: 'Howard did hire me to find Jim's killer.'

'I think Howard intended to alter the terms of the contract. Hiring you to find the killer in the first place might draw suspicion away from him.'

'Just the same,' Blade said, 'the men who nearly killed me are also likely candidates.'

'That's true.' She smiled at him. 'Now you know why my land is a treasure. The Spaniards came looking for gold, but if they had irrigated the land, they would have had a treasure beneath their feet.'

Blade said: 'Let me make a contract with *you*, Esmeralda. If you agree, I will break my agreement with Howard. I don't feel bound by it. He has done no more than use me.'

The girl asked: 'What kind of a contract?'

'To get you a modern legal claim to this land and to irrigate it.'

She laughed in her disbelief – 'But, my friend, I do not have that kind of money. It is impossible.'

'It's difficult,' he allowed, 'but not impossible.'

She became very still and looked into his face, saying: 'Everybody who says that to me wants something in return, more than I am able to give. What do you want, Joe?'

He put a hand on her shoulder – 'Maybe I want to build something. Most of my life I've been destroying something. Give me anything you want, girl. But you've already given me something I can't ever repay you for. A man can't pay adequately for his life.'

She took his hand from her shoulder and kissed it.

'Joe,' she said, 'I trust you like I trusted Jim. Enrique there will think I am a fool. Is that not so, *primo*?'

Enrique hawked and spat – 'No, *chica*. It is not so. I trust this man. He is a kinsman.'

She shrugged and laughed. 'See – the Santiago family votes for you by two-thirds. Come, now I will show you something else.'

Enrique took his gaze from the country for the first time and said: 'Esmeralda, we have been watched since we came to this place. There is a man with a glass on the ridge to the south of us.'

She turned her horse – 'We will go down to the *ojo*, *primo*. Hide carefully and see if we are followed.'

She and Blade made their way down a narrow trail on to lower ground, pushing slowly north along the line of the hills, travelling parallel to the verdant valley. Blade asked: 'What's growing down there?'

'Every kind of citrus fruit that you can imagine,' she told him. 'Mostly oranges and lemons. There are peaches there, too. Men say they never saw the like of them.'

'And you will grow the same?'

'Yes, but Santiago will grow everything it needs as well,' she replied. 'There will be cattle and horses. Now, you may laugh, I shall plant grass also. This land can support a hundred times the cattle it has now. This land here is good. All it needs is water. I have learned a simple secret. It is not enough for land to have water. It must also be well-drained. Let the water stay in your growing soil and it will grow sick. Enrique is a wise one. He can feel dirt with his fingers. He says our land is as good or better than the valley there. You watch, I shall people the land and the people will be fed by the land. There will be houses for them. They will all be proud to work for a Mexican. Can you believe that?'

Blade looked at her in admiration. There was nothing he liked more than true enthusiasm.

'Esmeralda,' he told her, 'I believe it. And I'll do my damnedest to see you get it.'

'There could be great danger for you.'

They were descending steeply now and began to edge their way between great boulders. A fresh breeze softly fanned their cheeks and, after a while they came down on to the flat where, to Blade's surprise, they found themselves suddenly in a small canyon.

It was one of the most beautiful places he had ever found himself in. The silver birch tree was king here. The graceful trees seemed everywhere except by the water and here the willows grew, dropping their graceful heads to the water. This water came from the *ojo*, an eye, a spring among the rocks. The music of it gently broke the silence of this rock-hewn cathedral.

'I always thought,' the woman said, 'that one day I would build a secret house here.'

Blade said: 'I had the same thought.'

'Joe,' she said, 'bring water to my land, make my claim good and this place is yours. Is that payment enough?'

'My God,' he exclaimed, 'do you mean it?'

'Of course.'

He grinned and held out his hand – 'We have a contract.'

She gripped his hand and said: 'I was never happier, nor more full of hope.'

He pulled her forward and kissed her. That kiss might have developed further, but there came a faint whistle and she snatched her mouth away.

'That is Enrique,' she said quickly. 'There is danger.'

There came a clatter of hoofs and a moment later Enrique rode into sight. As he came up, he told them: 'There is a man close behind me.'

The girl said: 'Come, let us ride. I do not want trouble.'

Blade said: 'Go ahead with Enrique. There is something I have to do under my new contract.'

'No,' she told him curtly. 'You do not know the situation here. You could get yourself killed. There are things I have not told you.'

She seemed genuinely scared, but he told Enrique firmly: 'Take your cousin, quickly.' Enrique knew an order when he heard it. He caught Esmeralda by the arm and told her to do as Blade said. She protested strenuously, but Blade put his quirt across the roan's rump and the little mare started off at a fast clip.

As soon as they had gone from sight, Blade rode his horse under the umbrella of the willows and quickly tied it. Then he ran into the cover of the brush to the north of the spring and disappeared from sight.

A moment later, a lone horseman trotted into view. Blade stayed under cover while the man rode down into the willows, gazed at the tracks there for a moment, and then swung down from the saddle to inspect them more closely.

Blade came from cover, remaining undiscovered by the dun horse that stood with its line trailing and struck it a hard blow across the rump. The animal gave a small squeal of alarm and ran twenty or thirty yards before it stopped.

The effect on the man was dramatic. He swung round still in a stooped position and faced Blade with a drawn gun in his hand. He looked for a second as if he were ready to kill, but at the sight of Blade standing there smiling, he relaxed slightly.

'I knew you were there,' the stranger said. 'I saw your horse.'

'Been blind if you didn't,' Blade said.

'That was a damn fool move,' the man told him. 'You could of got yourself killed.'

'Not a chance,' said Blade. 'If I thought you were trouble, you would now be dead as last week's mutton.'

The man looked affronted. He was a tall, well-set up fellow, tanned dark by the wind and sun, dressed in range clothes – California pants and wing-chaps, a Mexican jacket and a battered Stetson. The red kerchief around his neck had faded to a washed out pink. He looked like a fellow who could handle himself and anybody else on his trail.

Blade went on: 'But we're not shooting trespassers on Santiago land yet.'

'We?' said the man. 'Who the hell's "we"?'

'The Santiagos.'

'You mean the Mexes that claim this strip of dust?' There was derision in the voice.

'That's not the way I'd put it,' Blade said. 'Put up that gun and let's talk.'

'What's there to talk about?' The man did not show any sign of putting up the gun.

'Like why you're following Miss Santiago.'

The man looked surprised at the question – 'She was snoopin' on the Howard land. I kind of keep an eye on things.'

Blade said: 'I kind of keep an eye on things too, so we're liable to meet from time to time.'

The man allowed a slight but very cold smile to pull at the corners of his lips. 'Keep out of my road an' you won't get hurt.'

'That's nice of you,' Blade said. They were like two dogs sparring. Maybe bluff and threats would do in place of blows. Experience told Blade that the best policy was to establish his strength here and now. His last remark made the man suspicious, but he didn't act upon it. No further threat came. The fellow stood there, gun in hand, puzzlement beginning to show on his face. He was on the brink of a developing situation. Blade decided to push him over the edge, so he said: 'Now I'll see you back on to your own land.'

That solved all the other fellow's problems. Now he knew where he stood. He said pugnaciously: 'Like hell you will.'

'Like hell I *will*.' Blade nodded as if indicating something behind the man. 'Here's help on its way.' But the man refused to take his eyes off Blade. It was an old worn trick and he wasn't falling for it.

'I'm no pilgrim to fall for that one,' he said.

On the heels of his words, there came a light clatter of loose rocks as Enrique came riding back. Instinctively, the man briefly turned his head. Blade's right hand, smooth as silk, lifted the Colt from leather. Now the man's eyes were on Blade again and they became wide with wonder.

'Jesus,' he said.

Blade said: 'Drop it.' In theory he had no advantage over the man. They both held guns in their hands. But the speed of Blade's draw had given him a momentary ascendency. The man knew he faced a superior. The man dropped the gun.

'Mister,' he said. 'You're *some* fast.'

'I can't deny it,' Blade said modestly. 'Then, in my business, it pays to be fast or you're dead. Now, let's you and me swap names. Mine's Joe Blade. What's yours?'

'Lee Tolliver.'

Enrique rode up and leaned on his saddlehorn, watching.

'Well, Lee,' Blade said in a bland voice, 'this is the way the biscuit is browned, boy – I'm going to ask you a couple of questions and you're going to give me the truth. If you don't, I shall become unpleasant. If you prove really difficult, Ransome S. Howard will be paying terminal wages to a rider who won't ride any more.'

Enrique was grinning – 'I like this, Joe. For a long time I wanted to hear this said to that son-of-a-bitch.'

Blade showed his technique. He kicked the gun on the ground lightly as if it were nothing and said: 'Put the gun away, Lee. You won't be needing it.'

The man looked from the gun to Blade and slowly picked it up. He slid it back into its scabbard and stood there looking very foolish and a little mad. Blade put his own gun away and said: 'Enrique, you get along home. No call for you to waste your time on a little matter like this. There's nothing here I can't handle.'

'Sure,' said Enrique carelessly, as if he believed it. He turned his horse and rode away.

Blade said: 'Tell me about me being attacked in Kansas City and right here in these hills. Tell me about what you're searching for and think I have.'

Tolliver frowned and looked puzzled – 'I don't have no idea what the hell you're talkin' about. Honest.'

'I can always beat it out of you.'

'No, sir, that's what you can't do. You can't beat out of me what I don't have in me.'

'Well, I think I'll beat you just the same and see what comes out.'

Tolliver cleared his throat with care – 'I reckon you can't do that, Blade. You can try.'

The first parts of a man's body that warn of an impending attack are his eyes and his feet. Lee Tolliver's eyes signalled his intention as clear as a beacon, while his feet braced themselves on the ground. The blow he aimed at Blade's face, had it landed, would have been sufficient to fell a horse. Blade moved his head and gave it no more than a half-inch clearance.

Tolliver's drive forward brought him close to Blade, who drove his fist into the man's belly right up to the wrist. The upper part of the man's body snapped down and Blade hit him with the ball of his hand in the exposed neck. The man fell sideways and rolled over to gaze up at the sky. His mouth opened and shut in a desperate effort to get air into his starved lungs.

Blade waited.

Slowly, Tolliver rose to his knees. He raised unhappy eyes to Blade and said: 'This is only the start. This don't finish it.'

Blade said: 'So let's get on with the finish.'

Tolliver came to his feet in a rush. He didn't come upright, but drove at Blade with searching arms outstretched, no doubt planning to grapple with him and bear him to the ground.

Blade stepped aside and kicked his feet from under him. Tolliver hit the ground on his face, which did not do his face much good.

But there was some iron in the man. Howard had not hired a milksop. When he rose again, his hair was plastered to his face by sweat and dirt. Where the flesh showed pale, it was flecked with blood. He didn't speak, but came at Blade with some caution, like a man who has made a careful and accurate assessment of the opposition. He raised his fists and made a feint for Blade's head with his right. Blade moved his head to one side and went to move in, but was met with a lightning left that rocked him back on his heels and made him feel as if he'd had his neck broken.

In that moment, he knew that he had overestimated his strength. His days in bed now took their toll of him. Strength seemed to drain out of him as if by some evil magic. When Tolliver hit him under the heart with a haymaker from the right, he went down. Tolliver at once dropped on to his belly with his knees and knocked every last ounce of wind out of him. It was Blade's turn to gasp like a landed fish.

'See what I mean?' Tolliver asked, panting.

'Yeah,' said Blade. 'You made your point.' He tried to get to his feet. He got as far as one knee when Tolliver, ignorant of civilised rules, hit him again. Blade went down once more and this time he had the feeling that he was not going to get up. Tolliver laughed rather shakily and kicked him a couple of times. Blade felt as if every bone in his body was broken. Just the same, he was able to grab hold of an ankle when the third kick came. It was with enormous satisfaction that he watched the man go down slowly like a falling tree.

Tolliver hit dirt hard and Blade tried to get quickly to his feet and failed. He rose slowly to his hands and knees as the other man did the same. In that position, they knelt there and gazed mournfully at each other.

'Admit it,' Blade said, 'you don't have the strength to blow your nose.'

Tolliver gasped a couple of times and replied: 'You couldn't swat a goddam fly.'

'Watch me,' said Blade. 'I'm going to swat *you*, you son-of-a-bitch.'

Tolliver spat in derision and the effort nearly put him down again. Panting and wordless, they staggered to their feet. Tolliver started to drag his gun from its holster, but he had hurt his right hand and the task was difficult.

Blade hit him full in the face with a swinging right that was aimed at the jaw. Tolliver staggered back and managed to get the gun clear of leather. Blade kicked the weapon out of his grasp and, in doing so, lost his balance and landed flat on his back. Tolliver dove clumsily for the gun on the ground and Blade flopped towards him like a stranded porpoise. He got a grip on the man's wrist, but was quite incapable of preventing his picking up the gun. Slowly that gun came around to present its muzzle to him. But Tolliver had failed to cock it. He squeezed on the trigger and both exhausted men gazed at each other in amazement. Blade reached down, pulled his own gun from leather and tried to strike Tolliver on the head. He only succeeded in tapping him feebly on the shoulder.

'Oh, for God's sake,' Blade said in exasperation, and tried again. This time Tolliver rolled and Blade struck dirt.

Now Tolliver managed to cock the gun.

Blade cocked his own gun and fired.

Tolliver screamed as he was hit.

Slowly, Blade got to his feet. Physically, he felt terrible. He thought: *Esmeralda's going to nag me to death for this.* He walked over to Tolliver and looked down at him. The man gazed back at him with hurt eyes.

'You damn fool,' Blade said.

Tolliver muttered: 'You can say that again.'

Blade bent down and inspected the shoulder. He raised it from the ground and looked at the shoulder blade area. Tolliver groaned. Gently, Blade laid the man down again.

'I drilled you clean through the right shoulder, Lee,' he said. 'Thank your lucky stars I'm having an off day and didn't put one through the heart. What's it going to be – do we do a deal or do I leave you to bleed to death?'

The man thought about it for a moment and then said: 'I don't aim to die for wages, that's for sure.'

'All right – what do you know about this set up?' Blade asked.

'Nothing personal,' Tolliver said. 'A man tries to earn his keep, but that Howard don't work at gettin' loyalty.'

'That's a fact,' said Blade. 'I worked for him myself.'

Tolliver told him: 'You an' the Santiagos don't stand a snowball's chance in hell. Take some good advice and get out while the goin's good. You got big money working against you. Not just Howard. There's a local Texas big-wheel against you. A three-cornered fight.'

'Who's the Texan?'

'Raymond Glory.'

That took Blade's breath away. Here was somebody in the play he had not even contemplated. The fact that an outfit as big as Glory's was lined up against the Santiagos made him regret bitterly ever giving his word to Esmeralda. It was like signing his own death-warrant. The Glory ranches covered a large part of five counties of Texas. There were other holdings in Colorado and New Mexico. Glory could raise an army by lifting a finger. If he wanted Santiago land, it was as good as his. Not even Howard could raise the wherewithal to fight a family like the Glorys.

Tolliver was watching his face.

'I don't see you laughin',' he said. 'If you can ever raise a smile again, I'll tell you somethin' that'll wipe *that* smile off'n your face.'

'Go ahead,' said Blade, his heart sinking.

'Right this minute, they're cleaning out the Santiagos. When you get home, there won't be no home there, just some cinders and smoke.'

Blade went cold.

Hastily, he started to do something for the wounded man. He washed out the wound as best he could, tore the man's shirt into rags and bandaged the shoulder neatly. Then he helped Tolliver to his feet and fetched his horse.

'You did a good job there, Blade,' the man said. 'I heard tell you were a mean bastard. I'll tell in future you're a Christian mean bastard.'

Blade said: 'Lee, here's something else you can tell – neither Glory nor Howard are getting their hands on Santiago. They push it too far and they're going to have a full-scale war on their hands. If they want it any other way, they'll have to bury me and I don't aim to let 'em do that.'

Tolliver gazed at him in wonder.

'My God,' he said, 'I believe you mean it. You must have took leave of your senses. What in hell do you have to fight *with*?'

Blade laughed.

'Grit and credit,' he said. He helped the man on to his horse.

'I owe you one,' Tolliver said.

'Forget it,' Blade told him. 'Just put distance between us.' Tolliver grinned weakly, nodded and rode his horse away south.

Feeling considerably battered and shaken, Blade fetched his

horse and stepped into the saddle. He rode as fast as he could make it through the difficult country. Within minutes he had left the lovely canyon behind him. Within another half-mile, he came up with Esmeralda and Enrique. They had just turned to come back to him.

'We heard the shot,' the woman said. 'Are you all right?'

'Fine.'

'You don't look fine.'

Blade gave her his news – 'They're burning your place right now.' They both looked at him with startled eyes. Enrique exclaimed: 'Pablo!' They both reined their horses around and the next moment, they were all three riding at speed back towards the house.

8

They saw the smoke long before they came in sight of the plain. It was dark grey and it rolled up into the blue heavens like a flag of mourning.

As they came in sight of the house and saw the bright destroying flames, they saw that the men who had started the fire were still there. Small figures of horses and men darted across the scene. They could hear the faint, shrill cries of the riders.

They pulled in their heaving horses briefly. Plainly, the men below there thought they were safe. The act of destruction had given them a feeling of invincibility.

Enrique said desperately: 'Pablo must be dead. I know him. He would have fought them. You trusted him and he would not want to fail you. *Por Dios*, they were too many for him and my brother is dead.'

Esmeralda said quickly: 'Let us do nothing stupid. This is the time to do nothing. All they did is burn a house that is little more than a *jacal*. I shall build a fine house in its place. You shall see.'

Blade looked at her. She seemed amazingly calm.

'Enrique,' he said, 'take our cousin into the hills and we will meet there later.'

She caught him by the arm. 'What will you do?' Her calm seemed to slip.

'I'm not going to sit here while they burn your house down, that's for sure,' he said.

'What do they gain by burning a house? It is nothing. If

you go down there, they will kill you. You are worth more than a house to me.'

'Those men down there have the initiative,' he said. 'We must never let them have that. Now's the time to hit them, while they think they're winning. Those men most likely belong to Raymond Glory. Nobody ever shot their butts off. So there's a first time for everything. Those bastards are going to carry some dead home. Or you're finished right here and now.'

In a small sad voice, she said: 'I don't want men to die for me.'

'Maybe Pablo already did.'

He shook his arm free and spurred his horse forward. He heard her call out to him, but already his horse was sliding down the first steep incline, going down the very hillside down which he had crawled after he had been creased by the bushwhacker's bullet.

By God, he thought, *they're going to learn Blade's in this fight.*

When he reached the flat, he heard a clatter of hoofs and rocks behind him and, turning in the saddle, saw Enrique spurring after him. When the Mexican drew alongside, he asked Blade: 'What do you intend?'

'Cut 'em down to size,' Blade said.

They were spotted almost as soon as they hit the plain. Blade heaved his Winchester from under his left leg and jacked a round into the breech. Enrique followed suit. They did not slacken pace. Blade could see the figures of the men more clearly now, outlined starkly against the flames and the darkness of the billowing smoke. A man pointed. A few on foot were running for their horses.

'Just one thing, Enrique,' Blade yelled.

'What is that?'

'Don't get yourself killed – we need you.' He measured the distance to the old ruined stone cabin that lay between the hills and the burning house. He stabbed a forefinger in its direction. 'Us and the horses in there.'

They angled slightly and thundered to the ruin. Within a few seconds, they were inside and out of the saddle. Without another word, the two men got down on one knee and sighted on the horsemen. There were three within a couple of hundred yards of them, slowly cantering forward to see what they were up to. The two marksmen waited, allowing them to come within easy range.

The foremost of them halted his horse and bellowed: 'Who are you an' what do you want?'

Blade bawled back: 'Name's Joe Blade. I'm ramrodding Santiago and I want you dead.'

'You want me what?' the man yelled back.

'Dead,' replied Blade and shot him out of the saddle.

The other two at once reined in, but Enrique put two shots in their direction and one of them fell out of the saddle as lifeless as a doll.

The Mexican said quietly: 'It would be a pity if we permitted the third one to live, José.'

This other fellow was spurring away. Blade and Enrique fired two shots each. Horse and man came down.

Enrique said in a prayerful voice: 'Let them petition at the gates of heaven for the soul of my brother.' He looked at Blade sombrely and said: 'But you are a terrible man, Joe. I think we just took the war to one of the strong outfits.'

Blade stood up to gain a better view of the men near the burning house. They were gathered in a knot and a big man was talking to them. He turned and started pointing to different points of the compass. Blade hoped that the casualties they had suffered would make them pull out, but he was disappointed. He counted heads and found that six men were left on their feet.

Enrique hissed at him fiercely: 'Listen.'

Blade heard the sound of a speeding horse. He went to the

rear of the ruin and saw Esmeralda flat over the neck of her roan as it moved, fast.

'Doesn't that damn woman ever do as she's told?' he demanded of Enrique.

The Mexican said: 'Not ever.'

A moment later, they were helping her down from the saddle. Blade told her what he thought of her. Didn't they have enough on their hands without having a woman to protect?

She laughed without humour and said: 'You will have to protect that carrion from me, my friend. And you forget that I am the boss.'

'Well, keep your head down and don't start giving advice.'

She dimpled in a real smile now.

'I will give advice immediately,' she said. 'Both of you, be careful.'

Blade made a sound of disgust.

Enrique, who had returned to his window, called: 'Here they come. They intend to attack us from all sides.'

Esmeralda produced her own revolver and said: 'Three guns are better than one. I will watch the rear.'

Blade took a good look around. The ruined cabin was small and had been stoutly built. There was good protection here, but the ground all round was pretty broken and it would be possible for a man on foot to crawl within a few feet of the walls. The rear wall, away from the burning house, had been partly demolished. One rider was moving to a position between the hills and this unprotected rear. He joined Esmeralda.

'Sing out where each of them is, Enrique, and I'll do the same,' he said. 'We have one at the rear here. He's dismounting, so he'll be coming in on foot.'

'It's the same here,' the Mexican said. 'There are three on foot. There, they have disappeared. Joe, it is going to be warm in here.'

'Don't I know it. Esmeralda, can you shoot a rifle?'

'As well as you.'

'All right. Take this.' He thrust the Winchester into her hands and drew his Colt.

'What are you going to do?'

'I'm going out there.'

'That's crazy. You are safe here.'

It would be safe out there. The fellow coming in from the hills would not expect one of them to meet him halfway. Always take the fight to the enemy. This man had allowed Blade to see him, therefore there must be one or two others that he could not see. If Esmeralda used the rifle, they might think Blade was still in the ruin.

He touched Esmeralda's cheek with a hand and she gave him a faint, wan smile. Then he got down on his belly and Indianed out, rolling into a shallow gully and crawling along it. That done, he lay still and waited. He didn't intend to move until he had to.

No more than five minutes passed before he heard Enrique rip off three shots quickly.

Then silence took over again.

Another five minutes and he heard a whisper of sound. Cautiously raising his head above the rim of the gully, he was startled to see a man between himself and the ruin.

Esmeralda must have seen the man at the same time. Blade heard the sound of her carbine and her scream of warning. He cocked and fired the Colt once, saw the man throw up his arms and heard the roar of a gun behind him. He felt something tear through the sleeve of his shirt and flung himself down. The man behind him fired another shot and Blade heard Esmeralda levering and firing the Winchester. He could hear the slugs ripping through the brush.

Getting to his feet, he ran bent double and changed his position in the gully. Halting, he straightened up.

There was a man not twenty yards from him, kneeling and firing at the ruin. Blade fired and missed, but at least he succeeded in drawing attention from Esmeralda.

The fellow did not seem to make a break in his shooting. He simply swung around and started pumping shots in Blade's direction.

Blade ducked down and changed his position again. Turning an abrupt angle in the gully, he ran into near calamity in the form of another man. The only thing that saved him was that the fellow was as surprised as he was. Finding Blade right on top of him seemed to paralyse him. He crouched there, staring at Blade, who was so close that there didn't seem any sense in stopping.

They met almost head on. Blade's left shoulder barged into the fellow and knocked him from his feet. In falling, the man lost his gun, but that did not seem to deter him. He was apparently a good mover, for, as Blade turned to hold the gun on him, he dodged to one side, caught hold of Blade's wrist and hurled him against the side of the ditch. Blade lost hold on the Colt. He swung a fist for the man's head and missed. The fellow at once bent to pick up his gun, but Blade kicked him in the side and knocked him across the gully. Knowing that he could not regain his own weapon while the other was still on his feet, Blade hurled himself forward, hoping to bear the man down by sheer weight. But again the man moved quickly. He whipped aside so that Blade fell against the gullyside. As Blade fell, he received a boot in the belly. He lay there a moment, trying to recover himself, helplessly watching the man jump for the gun on the ground.

Knowing this to be his only chance, Blade launched himself on to the man's back. They went down in an untidy heap. The man rolled and hurled Blade from his back.

They both lay a second and the only sound in the gully was their panting breath.

Blade threw himself full length, stretching out his right arm to get his hand on the butt of his own gun. The man was on his feet, stamping down for Blade's gun-wrist savagely with his boot heel. But Blade managed to snatch his hand clear.

As he fired, the man was on him and he couldn't be sure whether he had hit the fellow or not. Certainly his attacker showed no sign of being weakened. He dealt Blade a couple of terrible blows and would have beaten him insensible with his fists had not Blade succeeded in bringing the barrel of the Colt down on his head. The heavy gun knocked the fellow clear, but it didn't put him out. He was having difficulty in focusing his eyes, but there was still a lot of fight in him. It took another terrible blow from the gun barrel to bring the combat to an abrupt conclusion. The man fell on top of Blade, limp and heavy.

With a supreme effort, for he was now almost helpless with exhaustion, Blade managed to roll the man off him. Then he staggered to his feet and stood there shaking. He took a look at the defeated man and saw that he was still alive.

Enough was enough, he told himself. The three of them should now call off the fight. This outfit would not forget what Santiago had done to them for a long while. Let them limp away and spread the word. Blade ran along the gully until he was opposite the rear of the ruin and climbed out.

He shouted as he neared the cabin, but there was no answering call. He experienced a sudden fear that the girl had been hurt.

But it was not Esmeralda who had been hurt, it was Enrique. He lay on the ground, trying hard to sit up.

'I am all right,' he was saying as Blade entered the ruin. Blade dropped on one knee beside the Mexican and found that his left arm was broken. He had lost a good deal of blood.

'It's time we went,' Blade told them. 'Enrique, if I tie a tourniquet around the arm, can you stay in the saddle for a while?'

'Sure. Hurry, I do not think our friends have had enough yet.'

Blade said: 'If not, they're crazy.' He took the Mexican's scarf and quickly bound the arm, using a small stick as a splint. Then he and Esmeralda heaved him into the saddle. When the girl was on her horse, Blade said: 'Don't stop for anything. Ride like the devil was after you – which is not far from the truth.'

However, his fears proved groundless. As they rode hard for the hills, there were a few shots from behind, but both the attackers and the three fugitives knew there was no danger of their being hit. When they had climbed into the hills and stopped to look back they saw a small file of riders going slowly southward. There were a couple of riderless horses.

'So,' Enrique said, 'there are at least two dead, though I suspect more. God rest their souls. But for us, that is good. These men will remember us.' And he added: 'As we shall remember Pablo.'

When they judged that the dust of the riders was far enough south, they ventured down from the hills. Now, they found Pablo, not dead, but wishing he were dead. He had been struck on the head by a gun and lashed to a hitch-post with a length of barbed-wire. He was not in good shape, but he was alive and for that they were duly thankful. He was dazed and confused and all he could think of was his need to apologise to Esmeralda for allowing the men to burn the house. However much she reassured him, he continued to apologise for the rest of the day.

Enrique seemed utterly disgusted that his brother was still alive. He appealed to heaven in his annoyance: 'Ignore the prayers I said for his worthless soul.'

When they went to the well to drink, they found that it had been fouled. This was all that was needed to cap a miserable day. They stood and stared mournfully at the last smouldering embers of the house. The old high-walled corral where a few spare horses had been kept was empty and this further depressed them.

'Well,' said Blade, 'where do we go now?'

Esmeralda did her best to give them a bright smile.

'Come,' she said, 'I will show you.'

What Esmeralda showed them was an old line-camp, high in the hills and out in the back of nowhere. Here there roamed half-wild cattle that hid in the thickets at their approach, long-horned beasts that fled as fast as deer for cover. This had been a camp for the line-riders in the days of Esmeralda's father. In those days there had been twenty riders on the Santiago payroll.

On the dusty shelves inside the building, they found ancient cans of beef which they ate hungrily off their knives.

The cabin was constructed strongly of squared logs and stone. Blade nodded approvingly. He reckoned it was strong enough to withstand cannon fire. It stood on a rounded grassy slope sheltered by timber that climbed to the tops of the surrounding hills. Not twenty yards from the door, there flowed a small creek. The corral of split poles needed a little repair and would serve their purpose.

When they were through eating, Blade and the girl attended to the wounds of the two Mexicans. Both men were cheerful enough and indeed seemed only glad that they were alive. Enrique seemed now willing to forgive his brother for not being dead as he had thought. Then Blade went out and did some repairs to the corral, using dampened rawhide strips to fasten the broken poles together. He threw the horses into the pen and saw that there was hay and water for them. Walking back into the cabin, he found that the woman had made the two wounded men comfortable in two of the bunks.

'Is this place known around these parts?' he asked.

'No,' Esmeralda told him. 'It has not been used for a good many years except when Pablo and Enrique come up here hunting. Maybe some of the old-timers who rode for my father know of it.'

Blade caught at the mention of the old-timers. 'Old timers, huh? How many men are there in these parts whom you could employ if you planted fruit on your land?'

She looked a little scornful at his foolishness. 'How could I employ anybody? The question does not make sense.'

'If you had the money – how many men?'

Pablo cut in with: 'There are many men.' He grinned. 'They are related to us one way and another. We all have one thing in common – we don't have ten cents between us.'

'Make me a list,' Blade said. 'I want to know where to find good men, men who will not break faith with you. We want workers, but they must also be capable of fighting if they have to.'

'I have told you,' the girl said fiercely. 'I don't have money.'

'Just give me the list,' Blade said. 'We have to do something or you will have no more land than you have money.'

While they were doing this, Blade went out again and looked over the horses carefully. He did so to give himself time to think as much as anything. He knew that he was going to take the gamble of his life. And he wasn't quite sure why he was going to do it. He knew that Esmeralda, as much as he admired her and thought her very attractive, was not the love of his life. Yet, for her, he knew that he was going to risk everything he had in the world. And maybe his life into the bargain. He must take after his old man – he didn't like to see people pushed around. That's why his father had died, he reckoned. At least there was no shame in what he planned. The only reason he could find in his thoughts was that he found it impossible to stomach injustice.

He thought about that, while he sat on the top-rail of the fence and smoked his pipe. He decided what he was doing was not such a damn-fool thing as it first looked. There wasn't much percentage in it, but it made living with himself a mite easier.

He chose a bay gelding, a sturdy unpretentious horse that seemed a little fresher than the others. It did not have much work left in it for that day, not after the hard climb, but Blade reckoned that beggars could not be choosers.

Back in the cabin, he found Esmeralda writing on the back of a canned beef label with a stub of pencil. She looked up at his entry and said: 'We have found you twenty good men. Some of them have wives – what about the wives?'

He grinned and said: 'If they're young I shall inspect them for suitability,' and she made a face at him. 'Find a few more. We'll need as many as we can get.'

'But the money,' she wailed. 'Where can we get the money?'

'That's what I'm going to do now,' he informed her. 'I'm going into Laredo to raise the money.'

She was on her feet – 'You could get yourself killed there.'

'I could get myself killed anywhere, but Laredo is the place to raise money.'

She looked dubious – 'I hope you're not thinking of using the land as collateral, Joe.' There was sudden suspicion in her eyes. 'It is not your land and you cannot act for me.'

'You don't trust me,' he said mockingly. 'I don't expect you to. But I'll show you that you can. Now, put a few more names down on that list and I'll hit the trail.'

'Luis Bandera,' said Pablo. His facial expression showed that he thought he'd come up with a jewel of a man.

But 'Tio Luis!' Esmeralda cried. 'Not for all the gold in the mountains. He is trouble, that one.'

Enrique said: 'There speaks a woman. Maybe we could do with one or two who are trouble. God knows that the other side have enough men who are trouble. Luis is good with a gun and the sight of blood is not new to him.'

The girl turned to Blade – 'Luis is nothing more than a *pistolero*. I will not have that kind.'

Blade said: 'Put him down.'

She stared at him for a moment, then shrugged. 'All right. But it is on your own head.'

When the list was complete, Blade tucked it in a pocket and said to the two brothers: 'You stay in one piece till I get back. And see your lady cousin stays that way too. We need her and her Spanish claim to the land.'

Esmeralda walked outside with him and watched him catch up the bay gelding. When he was saddled and ready to ride, she put her arms around his neck.

'Don't do anything to make me distrust you, Joe,' she said.

'Esmeralda,' he said, 'no good me arguing with you when you talk that way. You'll have to judge me by what I do. I'll make it so you keep that land. I'll put water on it and I'll make fruit grow on it. You'll have fat cattle on its grass.'

'Be careful in Laredo,' she said.

He kissed her and swung into the saddle. The sun was sinking and there was a cool breeze blowing from the north. He would be in town before dawn.

'Is there any piece of paper that says the land's yours?' he asked softly.

She was indignant.

'Of course. Why do you think there is all this killing?'

He smiled.

'Do you swear the land is yours?'

She held up the small cross of gold that hung from her neck.

'I swear on the cross,' she said. 'The land was my father's and my father's father's. It has been Santiago land back as far as men can remember. There is not a *paisano* in the country who does not know it. All you have to do is ask them. What do I have to do to convince you?'

'You just did,' he said.

He reined the horse around and lifted a hand in farewell. He rode off into the dusk. When he looked back, she was standing motionless by the corral, watching him.

9

Once in Laredo, Blade was a busy man.

Being also a man who liked to take things in their proper order, he took first things first. So, before doing anything else, he sought out an Italian barber shop, took a hot bath and enjoyed a shave. Thus civilised, he took a good Mexican breakfast in the shade of a stall near the waterfront. The proprietor was a pleasant Mexican lady of ample proportions and a nice motherly manner. They enjoyed a pleasant chat while he ate. Then he savoured a hot belch on the chilis and they both enjoyed another chat while he ate another breakfast.

The lady's name was Maria Lopez and she was married to a small skinny good-for-nothing fellow who was good for nothing but putting her in the family way. She was tolerant – every man to his own particular talent and he, it seemed, was particularly good at this. She had six children. It was good to have fine children, but her patience was wearing a little thin. She would stop at eight.

Her particular talent was gossip. She knew the talk of the town better than a good newspaperman. She rattled off names, and Blade's memory stored them away. She substantiated many of the statements of the talkative Italian barber. Blade paid her for the food, thanked her gallantly for her entertaining company and bade her good day. Then he strolled to the telegraph office and sent several very carefully worded wires.

His next visit was to the land agent's office, where he took the measure of the man and suggested that they do business over a convivial drink. Notwithstanding the earliness of the hour, the fellow gladly accepted and a small Mexican boy was sent for whisky. When the whisky was well down in the bottle, they were on first name terms and they were well down in business too. Ole Joe Blade was a real buddy, ole Harry Simpson could see that. Ole Joe was his kinda hombre. Ole Joe agreed, stuck a finger down on the map and said: 'I'm claiming this.'

Ole Harry Simpson nearly fell over the back of his chair.

'Jesus,' he said, 'you can't claim that, Joe.'

Blade rose, walked unsteadily to the door, locked it and pulled down the blind before he had reversed the notice that said: 'Back in five minutes.' He reckoned Laredo was accustomed to the land office being shut while ole Harry propped up the bar of the nearest saloon.

He came back to the desk and said: 'Harry, you ain't going to lose by this. I have plans and there's no reason on earth why you shouldn't be a part of 'em. If you're friendly.'

Harry's bloodshot eyes stared at him in something very like terror.

'I can't be friendly if I'm dead, Joe, you know that.' Harry's whisper was hoarse and shaking.

'You *could* be dead, if you stayed in Laredo,' Blade said. 'But with some good working capital, the world's your oyster.'

'You got that kind of money?' Harry asked in awe.

Blade nodded.

Harry thought about it. Avarice and fear fought each other all over his face. He looked around the office for advice, but didn't find it. He looked up at the ceiling in despair. Finally, he whispered: 'All right, I'll do it.'

'Have another drink,' Blade told him, pouring. Harry drank with more desperation than enthusiasm. 'Now I have some other claimants.'

'You do?' said Harry like a man beyond the expression of dismay.

'Yes, First, there's Pablo Santiago.'

Harry's jaw dropped.

'Christ,' he said, 'a goddam Mex.' He gulped and objected: 'He ain't a United States citizen.'

'Yes, he is. And so is Enrique Santiago, his brother, and so is Esmeralda Santiago, their cousin.'

Harry nearly fainted.

'Esmeralda?' he wailed. 'My God, I'm dead. You just killed me, you bastard.'

'Have another drink, ole Harry,' said Blade.

Next, Blade went to the bank.

Yes, said the proprietor, the marvels of modern communications had seen to it that Mr Blade's arrangements were made. Blade spent an hour with the banker and, when he was through, that gentleman walked with him to the street and was seen to bow politely to Blade by a good many of the citizens of Laredo. They were impressed. Old skinflint Carbody didn't bow to every Tom, Dick and Harry.

Blade next visited the gunsmith. This visit took up another hour. The gunsmith, Carl Luntz, came out on to the sidewalk and showed him every courtesy. Laredo was impressed again, because Dutch Carl was famous for his curt, not to say downright insulting, manner.

Blade then took his mid-day meal at the hotel where the Howards were staying and, as chance would have it, Howard and the ladies were at table as he walked in.

Heads turned when Blade cried out happily: 'Ah, there you are Mr Howard, ladies. A very good day to you.'

Howard turned his head and glowered in a kind of horror at the sight of him. The other absorbed diners watched with great interest. They saw that both ladies jumped as if they had been stuck by hat pins. They also observed that they first flushed scarlet, grew pale, then broke out into bright and happy smiles.

As for Mr Howard, he put on a performance that was sheer delight to the man-watchers. First, he grunted loudly and turned his head away from what was apparently the nauseating sight of Joseph Blade as that monster bowed to each of the beaming ladies.

'I hope I see you both well, ladies,' Blade said. And gave each of them one of those very special secret glances that were all the rage at that time. 'The sight of you both provides a fitting climax to a particularly wonderful day.'

Mrs Howard, first lowering her eyes modestly and then, just as modestly, raising them to Blade's, said: 'What can possibly be wonderful on a hot and dusty day in Laredo, Mr Blade?'

Blade cried, loud enough for every pair of ears in the diner to hear perfectly: 'Because I am alive, dear lady. Didn't you hear that the villains tried to assassinate me?'

'What villains, pray?' asked June.

Which was just the cue Blade needed.

'Why, the villains who attempted to seize the Santiago grant,' replied Blade. 'But this is not the kind of thing that ladies should be offered, as I am sure you would be the first to agree, Mr Howard?'

Howard was almost beside himself with rage.

'I have no wish for my wife and daughter,' he said, 'to converse in public with one of my hired hands.'

Blade smiled happily.

'Rest easy, sir,' he said. 'They do not. I am not in your employ. In fact, I ceased to be when you left me out there to die on that hilltop. No, I am now what you might call a landowner. I have decided to settle on part of the old Santiago grant.'

That brought Howard to his feet.

The little man used no more than a half-dozen words, but they were enough to send a shocked buzz around the diner. There were certain words that a man did not utter in front of ladies and he used most of them. His wife and daughter stayed very still in a stunned silence.

Blade raised his eyebrows. Having uttered those words poor Howard seemed as shocked by his behaviour as was everybody else present. But that did not lessen his rage. He was quite out of control and screamed at Blade: 'You're a low traitor, Blade. Get out of my sight.'

Blade said: 'If you want me out of your sight, Howard, you'd best turn your head away because I mean to eat here.'

With this, he bowed politely to the ladies, who gazed at him in bewilderment, raised a beckoning finger to a waitress and walked to the empty table on the far side of the room.

By the time another ten minutes had passed, during which he started eating with heads continually turning in his direction, it was his turn to be surprised.

A man sitting at the next table leaned over and said: 'It's none of my business, Blade, but I hate to see a man putting his head on the block. I just have to tell you Raymond Glory ain't goin' to be too pleased with you-all. You can't know the facts, or you wouldn't never claim on Santiago land.'

Blade nodded pleasantly.

'It's real kindly of you, sir,' he said. 'And I appreciate your gesture, but I am aware of Mr Glory's interest. In fact, it was brought home to me by one of his gun-hands shortly before I whupped him.'

The Texas cattleman who had addressed him, along with his three companions, leaned back in his chair and opened his eyes wide.

One of the other men said: 'No offence, Mr Blade, but you're either a fool or a brave man.'

'Neither, sir,' said Blade. 'I'm a businessman and I do not take kindly to anyone interfering with the healthy practice of private enterprise. Glory and Howard are trying to hog the whole range. It's they who are making the mistake as did the dozen men who burned Miss Santiago out yesterday.' The cattlemen looked uneasy and cast worried glances in Howard's direction. The man who had spoken first looked as if he wished he had not. Blade finished his short statement with: 'They burned the house and ran off the horses, but they also carried their dead away with them. They made the mistake all bully boys make – they underestimated the opposition. I never do.'

With that he resumed his meal, not doubting that before very long the scene in the hotel would be reported in detail (some of it exaggerated) to Glory.

While Blade was still eating, Howard and his two ladies departed from the diner. Neither Narcissa nor June looked in his direction openly, but both, as they passed him, managed to peek from under their long lashes at him. Each received a wink in return and each gave a pleased little smirk that was missed by Howard who walked ahead of them.

When he had paid his bill, Blade walked to the docks and chatted here and there with various characters. Thus, he located two men. One was Manuel Garcia, the other was Con McDee. With them, he repaired to a *pulquería* frequented by Mexicans, for they were both men who had tasted the *pulque* and had foresworn all other drink. When a bottle of this was set before them, Blade announced: 'I am about to make you both landowners.' It was the best opening remark he could make, for they were both landless men who pined for land. One was the son of an Irish squire who had ended his life in landless poverty, the other had lost his Sonoran acres to a land-hungry *ranchero*.

An hour later, they were in front of a greatly dismayed, but fortunately still drunken, Harry. The land agent almost wept when Blade told him what was demanded of him.

Blade said: 'I just had an idea, Harry. How about coming to work for me? We'll need a man who can read and write and keep records.'

'And get wiped out with you and the rest of your crew?' Harry said. 'Not on your life.'

Ten minutes later, McDee and Garcia walked out of the land office with land script in their pockets. They then accompanied Blade to some other addresses in town, where they found other men whose names were on Esmeralda's list. By the time Blade returned to the bank, he had recruited something like fifteen men. McDee and Garcia had meanwhile made their farewells, promising to meet with Blade the following day.

Now Blade moved with some trepidation, knowing that he was reaching a time of danger. To the best of his knowledge the affair was still a three-cornered one. In one corner was Howard – Blade didn't know how much force the man was willing to use. In another corner was Glory whose reputation was already well-established – he would behave as he always behaved, as though he owed nothing to any man and was above the law. As well he might, because there wasn't a sheriff in Texas who would move against him. While Blade was quite certain that Glory would move against him with guns in force, he wasn't quite so sure about Howard. Just the same, he would bear watching.

At the bank, he was received like visiting royalty. The bank owner rubbed his hands and said: 'Everything has been arranged for you, Mr Blade. You must forgive my – er – caution when you first visited here but . . . times being what they are . . . Now, I am entirely at your service.'

'Thanks. I'm doing deals with the gunsmith and the wagon-maker. The cheques for both will be considerable.'

Hands rubbed again – 'May I be bold enough to inquire, sir, just—?'

'You may,' said Blade. 'I am irrigating the Santiago.'

You could have knocked poor old Carbody cold with the proverbial feather.

'You have an arrangement with—?'

'Miss Santiago's interest is my interest.'

'But there are other interested parties, Mr Blade.' Carbody rolled his eyes at the very thought. 'Had I known when you first came in here, I would have warned you. I had no idea . . .'

'Your warning would have been wasted, Mr Carbody,' Blade said. 'I was already aware that both Howard and Glory wished to steal the Santiago grant.'

'Maybe "steal" is too strong a word, Mr Blade,' protested Carbody who was thinking of the Howard and Glory thousands deposited in his bank.

'No, sir,' said Blade, 'it is *not* too strong a word. Nor is murder too strong a word for what they have attempted. It's time Laredo revised its opinion of the two of them. A bandit is a bandit no matter how big he is.'

A short while after, as the sun began to sink again, Blade was at the freight yards asking for the owner. This turned out to be a Texas man by the name of Frank O'Neal. He was a bluff, tough and no-nonsense man who had freighted in and out of Texas along the old Southern Trail when a man had an Indian fight on his hands most trips. There wasn't much in life that scared him, except maybe a good woman.

Blade said: 'I'm hiring and buying wagons.'

'You've come to the right man,' O'Neal told him. Blade could tell from the man's amused manner that he had heard the news concerning Santiago. 'I build 'em and I loan 'em. Come into the office and let's do this civilised.'

'Doing it civilised' proved to be talking over a glass of whisky. It was good whisky and O'Neal didn't fool around, but got down to brass tacks right off. In response to Blade's questions, he said: 'I can sell you a good new wagon on the spot. Made it for a good friend of mine right here in town, but he ain't in no hurry. I can have another ready for you in four–five weeks. Meantime, I can hire you three with teams. Sell you mules if'n you want 'em.' He was a short, thickset fellow with clear bright blue eyes and definite movements. He cocked an eye at Blade and asked: 'Pay by cheque or cash on the barrel?'

'We can walk over to Carbody's and I can pay you cash right this minute.'

O'Neal said: 'We're in business. Have another whisky.'

'I'll want a teamster or two,' said Blade.

'I can find you a half-dozen.'

Blade walked around the freight yard, looking at wagons.

Satisfied that he was getting value for money, he made final arrangements with O'Neal and they walked to the bank together. Under Carbody's worried eyes, Blade paid O'Neal several hundred dollars as part-payment. Then there were handshakes all around and O'Neal said: 'It won't hurt this town to have somebody on Santiago that knows how to spend.'

Carbody said: 'Quite so,' but he didn't sound convinced.

Blade headed for the gunsmith's. Luntz had stayed open for him. The Dutchman had an eye to business and word had reached him that this man Blade was up against the big battalions. Such men had the habit of getting themselves killed with a surprising abruptness, so it was a wise precaution to get their money from them while you could.

The Dutchman knew that Blade was in the market for guns, but when he heard Blade's firm order, he was astonished. Even with an eye to business, he protested. It would mean that Blade would empty his store of weapons. Blade insisted. Nothing less than a dozen Winchesters would satisfy him and he wanted twice that number of Colt Frontiers to complement them. Then there was the ammunition.

The gunsmith made a little joke – 'One would think, Mr Blade, that you were going to fight a war.'

Blade said: 'That's what I intend, Mr Luntz.'

An hour later, he was at Luntz's door with his new wagon. Carl Luntz and his hired man helped him load the guns and ammunition.

The news went around town fast. When he reached the freight yard behind two spans of mules, O'Neal said to him: 'I hear you cleaned out Luntz's shelves.'

Blade grinned. 'I hope I clean Glory's plough as good.'

'Christ,' said Frank O'Neal.

'Frank,' Blade said, 'I aim to sleep on my freight tonight if that's all right with you.'

O'Neal returned the grin – 'Just so long as you stay on the far side of the corral. I don't fancy having my house burned down.'

So Blade slept with the guns that night and in the morning he was woken by McDee and Garcia. The two of them had brought supplies with them, so the three men cooked and ate their breakfast together. An hour later, they were joined by a dozen other men, Mexicans and Anglos. Not one of them, Blade knew, had either land or employment, and there was nothing like a lean belly to put some resolution into a man.

He made them a little speech as they squatted around drinking coffee.

'Men,' he said, 'you know how it is and I haven't tried to fool you. We're all in the same game. We make good or we fall on our fannies. If we fall on our fannies, we can only blame ourselves. You have to trust me and I have to trust you, because there's nobody else to trust. Now, let's rustle. We have to build another Santiago house by dark.'

Nobody said anything. Blade felt the men's eyes on him. He looked at the men. Here and there a man nodded. On the whole they didn't look an inspiring bunch. Blade faced the possibility of their not thinking him very inspiring either. They slowly rose and walked to their wagons, the drivers climbing on to their wagon seats and taking up their whips. Blade mounted a saddle-mule he'd bought from Frank O'Neal. The freighter walked up to say goodbye and to wish him luck. He asked: 'Any reason why you're riding a mule?'

Blade smiled.

'There's a reason,' he said. 'It's the outward sign of the new hard-working simple life I just started. No more dashing horsemanship for me.'

O'Neal laughed in disbelief – 'I don't believe it. Once a horseman always a horseman. Well, here's wishing you luck, Joe. I won't pretend you ain't going to need it.'

With that cheerful remark ringing in his ears, Blade led his little wagon train away from Laredo. The town watched them go. Even while the dust rose from the wagon wheels, there were men making bets on how soon they would be creeping back into town with their tails between their legs. That is, if they were still alive.

They had not covered a couple of miles when one of the drivers, a Mexican, called to him: '*Patrón*, there is a rider following us hard from town.'

Blade pulled to the side of the trail and saw that there was a lone horseman spurring hard after the train. A sudden premonition hit him and he put the mule into a brisk trot back down the trail to meet the approaching horseman. When the distance between had been reduced enough, he saw that it was Harry Simpson, the land agent. The man pulled his horse up in a lather. One glance at his face was enough to tell Blade that he was cold sober and in a high state of scare.

'My God,' he cried, 'you're the ruin of me, Blade. I'm finished. Why did I ever listen to you?'

'What happened?' Blade demanded.

'A whole bunch of bandidos attacked the land office. I was lucky to escape with my life. Those bastards came roaring up from Mexico like devils out of hell. They terrorised the whole goddam town and they burned down my office after they shot it up. How one of those slugs never killed me, I don't know. Why did I ever listen to you, Blade?'

He would have gone on all day, if Blade had not cut him short.

'Pull yourself together, Harry,' Blade told him. 'This isn't the end of the world. Maybe it's the best thing that ever happened to you. Did you get a good look at those Mexicans?'

Harry stopped and stared at him in amazement.

'What the hell did I want to look at Mexican bandits for?' he demanded. 'They were Mexicans. They're like Chinese. They all look alike to a white man, don't they? Hell, you know that.'

'I think one of 'em's been used before and I think some of 'em we'll see used again. I'm thinking of Jim Flaherty's death.'

'My God, you don't think—?'

'I think they were sicked on to you by Raymond Glory.' Blade looked keenly at him. 'I think that's what you think too. Else why're you boogered out of your skull?'

Harry went very still.

'Yeah,' he confessed. 'That's what I thought. But I'm a goddam mouse, Joe – you know I'm a goddam mouse. I couldn't face up to that. Christ, that's why I run to you. You said you'd give me protection. Right, I'm here. Give me protection.'

Blade grinned.

'I wanted you because you could be useful to us. All right, so you're here. Consider yourself protected. I have enough guns here for a small army. We're ready to take on anything and anybody. If we can't protect you, nobody can.'

If Blade thought that would comfort the man, he was mistaken. He just looked lost and hunted and said: 'I never heard of a man being protected against Glory. Did you?'

'Yes, me,' said Blade. 'And the Santiago brothers. We thinned Glory's numbers a mite.'

'You killed one of Glory's men?' Harry was hushed.

'More than one.'

Harry shook his head. His hangover hit him behind the eyes and nearly finished him. He groaned audibly and whispered: 'You're as good as dead, Joe.'

'Don't you believe it,' Blade said. 'If you can use a gun, get up there and help yourself to a Winchester out of the centre wagon.'

When they reached the site of the burned out Santiago home, Blade laagered the wagons and had a picket line formed for the stock. For the moment, he would not risk putting the animals out on grass where they could be run off by raiders. He had enough feed with him for a week. But he knew that he could not keep the animals off grass for long. He had just so much money, even though he had every cent of his own capital budgeted for, and as much more which he had on credit from a St Louis banker who trusted him. He had to go carefully or he would run himself into bankruptcy. And he had to work quickly, for he had to make good all the claims he had dotted about the old Santiago grant. Those registered claims which by now Glory would think had gone up in flames back in Laredo.

But first things first – with the old house replaced, they would all have a centre. A Santiago would be back in it and that would show everybody concerned, both on this side and among the enemy, what was what.

He sent six men, with a seventh to keep watch with a Winchester in his hands, to cut timber in the hills. They took mules with them to snake the logs down to the creek which ran about a mile from the old house. The new house would be thrown up on rising ground in a sheltered corner at the foot of the hills, just beyond rifleshot cover. There was water and grass there and two ancient cottonwoods. A good place for a house.

Some more men were set to digging foundations, following a rough plan hacked out of the ground by Garcia, who would oversee the building. Blade told the Mexican, who had built a house or two in his time, just how he wanted it. No time to make up adobe bricks. They would throw up a rough house of light logs. They had to be light because he did not want to ruin the mules snaking too heavy stuff from the hills. Then wet mud would be plastered inside and out. The roof was a real problem. There was no thatch handy. Shingles were out of the question because of shortage of time.

Garcia was not worried: 'I make flat Mexican roof, but not too flat. A man can fight from such a roof. You see. Have no anxiety in the matter.' Blade decided he knew what he was talking about, so he left it to him.

They did not get the house finished by dark, but the wood-cutters snaked in enough to start on the walls by first light. The foundations were dug and they would be ready to go as soon as it was light enough to see.

One of the men, Alonzo Díaz, had brought his wife along. Without the subject being mentioned, she became cook for the whole outfit. She fed them by firelight that night and had breakfast ready for them by dawn.

Blade said to Díaz: 'You married a treasure, Alonzo, did you know that?'

The man rolled his eyes and spread his hands in a kind of proud despair – 'I know, *patrón*. There are times when it is positively unbearable. She is as near perfect as I ever saw a woman. It breaks my heart she is so ugly.'

At dawn, the woodcutters hurried into the hills, hastening their mules with their sticks, their Winchester-toting guard watching over them. At the house, Garcia supervised the erection of the framework.

Blade found Harry Simpson still in his blankets. He did not stay there long. Blade stirred him urgently with his boot toe – 'Up. If you don't work, you don't eat. If you don't work after that, I throw you to Glory.'

Harry said: 'I believe you would too. My God, for a drink.'

'You can have a drink tonight when you've sweated yesterday's booze out of you.'

'Did anybody ever tell you you were a bastard, Joe?'

'Frequently, and better men than you.'

'I thought I hated Glory, but I hate you more.'

'That's a healthy state of affairs. Now get working.'

'I didn't eat.'

'You eat at noon.'

'I quit.'

'You can't, it ain't allowed.'

All in all, Harry Simpson worked well that morning. By noon his hands were blistered and his back and limbs ached enough to be Indian torture. Blade told him it would be worse tomorrow. Which he took in good part.

'You know, Joe,' he said, 'I feel pretty damn good. Maybe this is what I missed all these years. Maybe I wasn't meant for a desk job.'

Blade had a word with Garcia. Was there a man who knew the hills well? The Mexican nodded. There was True Prescott – he was the little ornery dried-up fellow in leather pants. Long ago, he rode for Old Man Santiago, Esmeralda's father. He knew all this land, including the hills, like the back of his hand.

Blade approached the man and told him what he wanted. He was to find Esmeralda and bring her and her cousins down to the new house. She must be guarded well and she must arrive safely.

'Don't you fret none, boss,' said the old man. 'I'll get her down here.'

He took a small roan Spanish horse and rode off into the hills, his shiny new Winchester hanging from the saddlehorn.

Blade experienced a sudden feeling of elation that took him by surprise. This was something he had never known before. He was building something. He looked forward to seeing Esmeralda's face when she saw her new home. The men were singing down at the creek where they were gathering rocks to build the chimney. Garcia announced that he was going to build the best chimney ever seen in these parts.

'There never was,' he said without false modesty, 'a man who could build a chimney as I can. For generations, they will point at it and say: 'Look – there is a Garcia chimney.'

The rocks clunked into the bed of the wagon. Blade saddled the mule and rode to check on the woodcutters. He found them hard at work. Triumphantly, they showed him a longhorn steer they had roped and lashed to a log. He inspected the animal and saw on it a brand made up of a highly decorated S. So they were going to eat Santiago beef. Tonight, they would have good red meat to stick to their ribs. He stayed with the men, using an axe and enjoying the strenuous work. When they headed back for camp, snaking logs, he put his own mule to the work. Mrs Díaz made joyful sounds at the sight of the steer. Within minutes the unfortunate beast was slaughtered and butchered. Men honed their knives to skin it, and cut what meat they could not immediately use into strips for drying into jerky. Some cut their beef into scallops and cooked them on sticks over the fire. It was quite a feast. Somehow there seemed something to celebrate. The frame of the house was up and the timber part of the walls in place, the plastering had begun. Garcia was halfway with his chimney.

'The best goddam chimney you ignorant *paisanos* ever saw in your miserable lives,' he said.

His partner, Con McDee said: 'Garcia, you're fuller of shit than any Mex I ever saw and then some. Which is saying something.'

'Could you do better? Are there better chimneys in Ireland from which men like you flee at the smallest chance?'

McDee said: 'One question at a time. First, I came all the way across the ocean to this God-forsaken land to bring Irish civilisation to you poor benighted Mexes. Right? Right. Chimney? Hell, I don't waste my time on chimneys. I build *houses*. While you been putting one itty-bitty rock on another, I been building a *house*. You reckon this here Señorita Santiago is going to notice a goddam chimney when she can admire my *house*?'

'You built it under my instruction and orders,' said Garcia, sticking out his chin. 'I did not hear you consulting with the *patrón* on the construction of the house. Or maybe that's because nobody can understand a mick which talk like a goddam foreigner.'

They worked on by the light of the fires and then old Prescott came in with Esmeralda and they all gathered round to greet the traditional owner of the land. They smiled and nodded. Some of the Mexicans pulled off their hats and Mrs Díaz, who had known Esmeralda some time in the past, came up and kissed her with a warm embrace. Even Harry Simpson, who seemed convinced now that he was some gallant hero on a magnificent crusade, came to shake her by the hand, declaring that they were devoted to her cause to a man.

Esmeralda was delighted and confused by it all. The sight of the house overwhelmed her and all she could say in Spanish was: 'My friends, my friends . . .' For a moment, it seemed that Blade's part in it all was overlooked.

But she came to him beyond the circles of light from the fires when the hubbub had died down. Her voice was very soft when she said: 'You did all this for me, Joe.'

'Not all for you, Esmeralda,' he said, 'for myself also.'

She seemed at once to misunderstand him. Her voice was suddenly cold and hard – 'I heard from Harry Simpson that you have claimed Santiago land.'

'I can explain that,' he said.

'How can you explain that some of my land is now in your name?' she snapped. 'I warned you. I shall contest it. I still believe that when the time comes the court will recognise the Spanish paper.'

He said: 'It's an old trick used by big cattlemen all over. They are allowed to claim only so much land personally. So their hired hands claim it for them. When it's proved up, their hands sell it to them for a token sum. If the Spanish paper holds good, you have nothing to fear, any road.' He took the scripts from a pocket and handed them to her. 'That's what I've done. You, your cousins and several of these men have claimed land. I have checkerboarded the whole Santiago country and cut off the main accesses to water. I don't know why you didn't think of it before.'

She laid her head against his shoulder.

'You will think me a terrible distrustful woman, Joe,' she said.

'I don't think anything of the kind,' he said. 'You're making a fight of it. Nobody can ask more than that from you.'

'And where does all the money come from to pay the men, to pay for the wagons, the guns and the supplies?'

'Let's say there's some have faith in the future of Santiago.'

'In other words, you could bankrupt yourself for me,' she said. 'I know you are not a rich man.'

'I shall be paid,' he said. 'You promised me the canyon.'

She laughed and said: 'I think you are planning to marry me, you scheming devil, Blade.'

'No,' he said. 'I'm not planning to marry anybody.'

She kissed him and said: 'There's a man who knows his own mind. I think I should feel insulted.'

'There's no insult in ten thousand acres of fruitful soil. Right across here and on the far side of the creek will be a settlement. There will be sheep and cattle in the hills. Men will come from all over to see what can be done by bringing water to a thirsty land.'

'You're a strange man,' she said.

'Crazy's a better word,' he told her.

The house was habitable the following day, and by the evening Mrs Díaz cooked her first meal in the kitchen that had been tacked on the east end of it. Blade told Esmeralda that he planned to extend the building later so that it stood on an oblong patio.

The work had done one good thing beyond the construction of the house – there was already a sense of community among the men. Now Blade knew that the time of real risk had come. If Glory knew his business, he would wait to strike at the Santiago people after they had scattered and it was now time for them to spread out over the country. Blade started to tell the men where they should stake their claims and slowly they were allocated wagons and began to move to their new locations. Where possible, Blade tried to pair off the more aggressive types with the milder. He made sure that there was a Winchester repeater with each party. Old Prescott headed into the hills again and this time brought down Enrique and

Pablo. Neither of the two men were fit for hard work or riding yet. The journey down from the hills had been painful and difficult for them. However, they could sit in the shade of the new house with their rifles in their hands. With Simpson and McDee, Esmeralda started round the country to recruit men for the digging of the irrigation ditches. Blade thought her physically safe enough. He doubted if even men of Glory's evil reputation would harm a woman.

Blade's plan was to give the men who were staking claims a week to build themselves some kind of shelter and settle in. These claims were for the most part along the creek. As soon as they were settled, they were to start digging ditches from the creek along lines which Simpson would work out for them. Harry's knowledge of the land would come in handy there. Blade knew only too well that this was work for an expert, but he didn't have the money for an expert and there were certain chances that he would be forced to take.

'Harry,' he told Simpson, 'if you haven't worked it out so water flows down hill, I'll make you drink water all the time you're on Santiago.' But Harry was drinking less hard liquor. Sure, he emptied a bottle most evenings, but he didn't seem able to find time during the day. In fact, for hours at a time now, he forgot about drink.

Esmeralda said to Blade: 'That Harry Simpson is a gentleman, Joe. I like him.'

That surprised Blade. He thought Harry was a drunken bum, whose only assets were an ability to read and write, but he could be mistaken.

Now Blade started to ride the country, checking water sources, checking grades, checking on how the work on the scattered homes were going. He realised that for days now, he had not thought of his physical condition. Like Harry with his drinking, there had not been time.

10

On the seventh day, Howard came to the house with Chard and demanded to talk with Esmeralda. But she was not there. She was out stomping the country in search of recruits. So Howard had to be content with Blade. Though he wasn't too content, as was pretty evident. The fact seemed to choke him and only the urgency of the situation prevented him from raging away from the place back to Laredo with his pride in his pocket.

Mrs Díaz brought the visitors lemonade. She served them with exquisite Mexican courtesy and Howard ignored her.

'I'll get right down to business, Blade,' he said. 'I'll buy you out. With Esmeralda or without her. I want this land. You know damn well your checkerboarding will not hold water in any decent court.'

'Checkerboarding plus the Spanish grant,' Blade told him.

Chard sat silent with a long face, listening and watching.

'Not to put too fine a point on it,' Howard went on. 'I mean to have this land no matter what. Man, *you* can't develop it. I know you don't have the resources.'

'My bank has the resources,' Blade said. 'After the first crop, I shall have more than enough. I have willing workers. I have guns.'

'You may as well make up your mind to the fact that I shall have it,' said Howard, not at all put out. 'Be a realist. Better a sure thing than a gamble.'

'Not so much a gamble as you think,' Blade said. 'On good information, I know that Glory intends to stop you in your tracks, Howard. For some crazy reason he seems to fear you as much or more than me.'

'Glory does not even know that I want the land,' Howard said.

'If you believe that,' Blade informed him, 'you'll believe anything. Glory went after me in Kansas City because he knew I was working for you. I have made sure that he knows you and I are not keeping company now.'

Howard stayed an hour, arguing with increasing venom, but to no purpose. As his realisation of defeat increased, so did his rage. Finally, he shouted: 'I will not vouch for the safety of any man, woman or child on Santiago. Don't say you haven't been warned.' He stormed off to his buggy.

Chard shot a cautious glance after his employer, then said softly to Blade: 'Watch your back, Blade. It's no holds barred from here on in. Get Esmeralda out of it.' With that he stalked after Howard. Blade watched them drive off.

Then he went to look for the signals. This was a system of reporting in by the scattered units that he had instituted. Each night before sunset, the men lit green fires and sent a smoke signal. A simple column of smoke untouched if all was well, broken several times if help was needed. Tonight, the signals went up as usual. Most of them, Blade could see from the house. Two or three were relayed across the country from the direction of the hills. Only one to the north-east could be seen from no other place than the first ridge of the hills. A young boy, Juan Batista, went each night to check on this one. For this purpose, he rode a rawboned half-wild mustang. Tonight, he came racing this animal back to the house.

'There is no signal from Esteban Morales, *patrón*,' he told Blade.

'You waited sufficient time?' Blade asked and the boy nodded. Blade told him to saddle his mule. He told Mrs Díaz what he was going to do. He expected Esmeralda back that night.

He took the boy with him to the north-east. The claim to which he rode was one being worked by Esteban Morales, a steady and sober Mexican, a landless farmer. He was partnered by a younger man, Jesus Ruiz. Before riding on, Blade checked once again from the ridge that there was no smoke to be seen. The ridges to the north-east were smokeless. The mule hammered its way along the narrow trails, climbing steadily.

As they came to the claim, they saw smoke. They knew this was not any signal fire. The cabin built by Morales and Ruiz was burning. Almost as soon as they spotted the smoke, they were fired at. Blade guessed there were two marksmen high in the rocks and that they had probably taken up their position for just this purpose. He retreated with the Mexican boy and dismounted in the cover offered by thick timber. He knew that his signalling system was known to the enemy. They had burned the cabin and maybe killed the two occupants. They had waited for him to come riding in, but somebody had got too excited and fired too soon.

'Juan,' he told the boy, 'ride back to the señorita and tell her what has happened. Let two more men, if they will, come up here to rebuild the cabin.'

The boy rode off. Night was almost on Blade now. He doubted the enemy would stay at the claim after dark, but he decided to take no chances. He scouted the cabin pretty carefully until he was sure that the two marksmen had ridden on.

He found the ditch the men had started to dig. Already they had a channel running steeply west towards the plain two or three hundred yards long. They had worked hard and fast.

He found the dead body of Jesus Ruiz in the ditch. He had been shot between the shoulder blades and the back of his head. There was no sign of any weapon near. Blade stood and stared at the body for several minutes, suffering his own bitter thoughts, knowing that if it hadn't been for him the man would still be alive.

He started the search for Esteban Morales, fearing the worst. After a while he called his name several times. At last, he found him lying unconscious among the trees. It looked as if he had crawled there and hidden from the attackers. Blade, going by the fact that the man's Winchester was beside him, reckoned the enemy had not found him. Blade toted him to the nearby creek and poured the clear mountain water down his throat. Almost at once, Morales choked and slowly came round.

He was in an acute state of shock, but Blade knew he would live.

'There were six or seven of them, Joe,' he said. 'We put up a pretty good fight, but Jesus was killed and I was hit in the arm. I guess I lost a lot of blood. Jesus was a good man, Joe.'

He passed out again after that. Blade bound the arm as best he could in the poor light and thought he had stopped the bleeding. It must have been midnight when he heard the riders. By this time Morales was declaring that he was fit to ride. The riders proved to be Esmeralda with True Prescott and Garcia.

The girl had known Jesus Ruiz for many years and news of his death shook her, but she was pretty steady. The same thought that had troubled Blade troubled her. How many men's lives could be spent on a project such as this? Was it worth human lives? She put it to Blade and he replied: 'These men know what they're taking on. All I can promise is that I shall do what I can to stop the killing.'

They had brought fresh horses for him. Blade said he would keep Prescott with him if the old Texan would care to risk his neck, while Esmeralda and Garcia took the wounded man back to headquarters.

Morales said: 'I will rebuild the little house, Joe. Two days and I will be fit again.'

Old Prescott said: 'Let's sleep on it, Joe. We'll pick up their sign in the morning. But they'll be back at Glory's place by noon tomorrow.'

Esmeralda said: 'You won't do anything dangerous, Joe, will you? We don't want any more dead men.'

'Bank on it,' Blade told her blandly. But he knew he was lying. Destructive rage was eating at his guts.

She kissed him and rode away into the night. Blade and the old man dug a deep grave and planted Ruiz by moonlight. Prescott said a few words over him and that was that.

Blade and Prescott were awake before dawn and eating breakfast by first light. Blade's fresh mount was a stout, long-winded dun gelding that looked as if it would run all day on a handful of grass. The old man said with a cackle of admiration: 'The little lady sure do know horses.'

They were saddling their animals when they discovered that Glory, or whoever, had not lost interest in them. Somebody in the rocks above them shot Prescott's horse through the head and it fell dead. Blade and the old man dived for the trees and hugged cover as if it were a lover. The men above fired some more, this time at the dun, but the horse followed them quickly into the trees. It at once settled happily to cropping the grass there.

'Joe,' old Prescott said, 'I never saw a man kill a horse like that before. There's sure one sick bastard up yonder.'

Blade asked: 'How many do you reckon?'

'My guess is two,' the old man replied. 'One with a Winchester, the other with a Ballard. It was the Ballard shot my horse. An' I'll tell you-all somethin' for nothin' – before too long I'm a-goin' to blow the head off'n the son-of-a-bitch that killed my horse.'

'Stay right here,' Blade told him. 'Make a noise like two men. Call out every now and then.'

'Keno,' said Prescott. There was a kind of fierce happiness in the old man now, as if the shooting had somehow brought him fully alive.

Blade worked his way through the trees, going north. He went with great caution because the lie of the land told him that, if the bushwhackers knew their business, one of them would be trying to outflank the two Santiago men among the trees.

He was right. As he was slipping along a gully strewn with rocks and brush, he heard a light rattle of loose rocks and saw a figure moving slowly above him. Blade let the man pass him and at once started to stalk him. The fellow led him back into the trees and there, well out of sight of the other man above, Blade caught him flat-footed and braced him.

The fellow was youngish with the hard features of a professional gun-hand. The rifle in his hands was a Ballard. Blade took the rifle from him, turned him around and hit him with the butt of his Winchester. He then caught hold of him by the bandanna and dragged him back to True Prescott.

The old man took just one look at the man and the rifle and said: 'What I tell you? He done it with a Ballard.' He slapped the gunman's face until he came round and said to him: 'You kill my horse, punk?'

The gunman sneered silently at him.

The old man got so mad at this that he hit him and knocked him unconscious again. Then they put a rope on him and lashed him to a tree.

They were just through with this chore when a voice said: 'Grab sky, fellers.'

Neither being greenhorns, they obeyed instantly.

The man who held the gun was of the same breed as the man who lay tied to the tree. His eyes showed as much sympathy as a piece of rock.

He said: 'If the boss didn't say bring you in alive, Blade, you'd both be dead right now. We'll take the old rooster along for good measure.'

'You ain't takin' me nowhere,' crackled old Prescott. 'So save your fool breath.'

'You, Blade, unhitch my partner.'

Blade released the man he had just tied. He was feeling sick at heart and foolish. He also knew with a horrible clarity that his capture could mean the end of Santiago. Not that Esmeralda and the others were not capable of carrying on without him, but that, once he was in Glory's hands, the girl could be blackmailed into defeat. Glory would drop him down a deep hole if the girl went ahead.

So, he told himself, it was now or never.

He glanced at True Prescott. The old-timer looked as calm as it was possible to be. He might have been at a Sunday meeting.

From under his eyelids, Blade checked on the position of the man with the gun.

The man he had just released was starting to come round, groaning faintly.

Blade flicked the rawhide *reata* which they had used to tie the unconscious man. The line snapped forward like a striking snake, cracking into the gunman's face.

The man's professional reaction was instantaneous. His thumb wrenched back the hammer and his forefinger pressured the trigger. The heavy gun roared.

Already old True Prescott was moving, diving full-length for the Winchester on the ground. Blade's right hand slapped down on the butt of the Colt that still hung at his hip.

The gunman immediately fired a second shot, but the rope in his face had confused him. The end of it had caught him in the eye and he was half-blinded. The bullet hit the dirt not an inch from the old man.

Blade's bullet caught the fellow high in the body.

Before Blade could fire a second time, Prescott had the Winchester in one hand and had fired first. The bullet caught the gunman in the head and killed him instantly. Dead on his feet, the fellow spun round and dropped to the ground.

The other man sat up and gazed at the scene as though he could not believe the evidence of his eyes.

'Aw, my God,' he said indistinctly.

Blade and the old man stayed very still, staring at the dead man.

True Prescott said, with a kind of sad regret: 'I killed the wrong man. But there's still time to plant the other bastard.'

'No,' said the surviving gunman. 'Christ, I only work for wages.'

Prescott climbed stiffly to his feet and said: 'What kind of excuse is that, for Christ's sake, dumbhead? You boastin' you killed my good friend Jesus Ruiz for goddam wages, you yeller-bellied son-of-a-bitch?'

He looked so poisonous, the gunman yelped to Blade: 'Keep the old fool off'n me, will you? Likely my skull's broke. I could die.'

The old man yapped: 'You bet your sweet life you could.'

They tied the man up again. He seemed too unnerved to be any kind of opposition to them. Blade told Prescott to keep an eye on him while he went in search of the men's horses.

He found them fifteen minutes later, tied in high timber. They were excellent animals. He led them back to the old man and said: 'True, how do you feel about guiding me to Glory's headquarters?'

The old man cackled happily.

'That was always my aim,' he said. 'Sure, I'll go along. But we don't want the stiff and this jailbird along.'

'We're giving 'em back to Glory,' Blade told him.

Prescott looked at him as if to check he really meant it. He saw that Blade's mouth was set and his eyes were terrible. Not long after, they were on their way.

11

They went to Glory's place by the back-trails. Sometimes they left the often faint trails altogether and worked their way through rough country. They moved unerringly, for old True Prescott remembered all he had learned around those parts when he was a young rider on Old Man Santiago's payroll.

They eased into Glory country quietly, using all the cover they could so that all Blade had to do to reach the house was to cross three hundred yards in the open. He said to the old man: 'True, give me two hours. If I'm not back in that time, you high-tail it home. I mean it.'

'Sure, you mean it,' Prescott said, 'an' that's just what I aim to do. You go ahead now.'

Blade headed down out of the deep brush that covered the last ridge above the house. The bound man and the dead man were on one horse and the animal did not like either the double burden or the fact that part of it was a dead man. The prisoner was not too happy about the dead man either.

Blade went in slowly to the house and the Glory men were ready long before he reached there. There was no show of violence against him, no indication that they intended taking him prisoner. It was plain to see that he had no intention of going anywhere but the house. He certainly had no intention of evading them.

As he rounded the first split-pole corral, he started along the length of what looked like the bunkhouse. Several men had come out to watch him. There was no friendliness in their eyes. But he had not expected any. As he passed them, they started after him, walking their short-paced, choppy horsemen's walk on their high heels. There was another building before the big house. From it came two men and they had carbines in their hands. Blade did not so much as turn his head in their direction. He reined in the dun at the hitch-rail in front of the house.

Two men walked out on to the lower gallery.

One of them was short and powerfully built. The other was lank. The first was Blade's age. The other was twenty years older. The short one did not wear a gun, the other packed one low on the left side so that the butt was on a level with his hand. They both had handlebar moustaches, one ginger, the other grey.

The short man said: 'You have to be Joe Blade.'

Blade nodded – 'I don't know who you have to be, but my guess is you're Glory.'

'Folks call me "Mr Glory".'

'That's nice for you,' Blade said. 'I have a dead man here and he bears your brand. The fellow who looks like he ate a bale of bob-wire doesn't have too much enthusiasm for your service right this minute.'

Raymond Glory's facial expression did not change. He made a small sign with his hand and several men hurried forward to lift the dead man from the horse and to release the prisoner.

Glory said: 'Well, Blade, I have to admire your gall. Now, you didn't ride in here just to bring me back a failure and a dead man. Why're you here? It strikes me you must think me a fool.'

'I'm here,' said Blade, 'because I'm sure you're not a fool. You would rather make a deal than have any more killings.'

'It ain't my habit to negotiate,' said Glory. The face was mild and half-smiling, but the eyes were as cold as agate.

'It would be wiser to talk than to shoot this time,' Blade said.

'What makes this time different?'

'Me.'

'But you're here, and out-numbered twenty to one,' Glory said.

Blade said evenly: 'If that's the way you see it, go ahead and see where it gets you.'

The short man looked at the lank man, who said laconically: 'Let's talk. Talk costs nothin'. Maybe he has somethin' to offer.'

Glory said: 'Step down and come on in.'

Blade dismounted and tied the dun. The two of them led the way into the house, the lank man's spurs jingling musically. They entered a large hall with several rooms leading off it. Glory lived in real style, as Blade had expected. But he did not expect the woman who appeared in the doorway of one of the rooms.

'Why, Joe Blade,' she said mockingly.

June Howard looked as lovely as he remembered. She leaned gracefully on the door frame. Her hair shone like bright gold, her eyes were as unbelievable as ever. She was still one of the most magnificent women Blade had ever seen.

'I didn't expect to see you here, Miss Howard,' he said.

She smiled – 'Father and Mr Glory did a deal.' Blade glanced at Glory. The bland expression of his face had surrendered to one of rage. 'They plan to split Santiago right down the middle. When they have that settled, no doubt they they will turn on each other.'

Something sang a little song in Blade's head. The girl was still an ally of sorts. Maybe this was the only way she could get the warning message to him.

He said to Glory: 'I thought you never negotiated.'

'Women,' said Glory through his teeth, 'talk too damn much.' He led the way down the hall. Blade gave June a grin as he passed her and she blew him a kiss.

Glory entered a long narrow room at the rear of the house. It was tastefully furnished in half-Texan half-Mexican style – colourful rugs, cowhide chairs and one or two good paintings of men and women whom Glory no doubt claimed as ancestors. There was a long table of Spanish oak. The lank man pulled out a chair and sat down. Blade followed suit and asked: 'And who might you be?'

'I'm Phil Larson.' The man showed no annoyance at the question. When Blade heard the name, he knew why the man was so calm. He had no reason to be anything else.

'I heard of you,' Blade told him.

Who had not heard of Larson? A mild-mannered and terrible man who should have been hanged long ago back in the days of the early trail-drives. He had used that gun too skilfully and too often for the comfort of lawmen in the service of the Glory family.

Raymond Glory lit a large cigar and puffed smoke into the still air.

'Shoot,' he said.

Blade leaned his left arm on the table and let the silence take over for a moment.

'You've killed your last man on Santiago,' he said. 'I've heard tell you've fought a good few wars in these parts, in Colorado and up in Montana. That's because you never had any real opposition. You come against Santiago again, Glory, and all the fast guns you can buy won't stop me from burning this place to the ground.'

Glory laughed. It was not a pleasant sound.

'My God,' he shouted, 'it ain't gall you have, Blade. It's plain old-fashioned dumbness. I can take Santiago tomorrow, just like that.' He snapped his fingers almost in Blade's face. 'You're all wind and piss, man. Just like I thought. You don't have any deal to make. Not any kind. You're just bluffing.'

Blade said: 'I didn't finish. When I've burnt the house, I'm going to pick you and your crew off one by one. I'll kill every damn one of you if you touch Santiago again.'

Glory bellowed, 'Bluff,' in Blade's face.

Phil Larson said quietly: 'Not this one, Ray.'

'What?' Glory swung on his henchman in undisguised astonishment.

'Blade's been here before,' Larson said. 'If he says he'll burn this place and whittle us down, it don't mean he can do it. But, by God, he'll have a goddam good try.'

Glory snarled at him: 'Whose side you on, for crissake?'

Larson said: 'I didn't think that was ever in doubt.'

Glory stared at him for a long time as if he waited for the old gunman to modify his opinion of Blade. Finally, he turned to Blade and said: 'All right, what's your deal?'

'Compensation for the dead man's family,' said Blade. 'Let's say one thousand dollars. Compensation for burning down the house—'

Glory hit the table with a fist.

'When I say "deal",' he shouted, 'I mean: "what're *you* offerin' *me*?" '

Blade showed surprise.

'Offering you?' he said. 'Why I just told you. I'm offering to burn this place down, to eliminate you and your crew.'

Glory was apparently struck speechless for a moment. Slowly he mastered himself. He went to speak, but before he could utter a word, Blade pushed at him: 'You're thinking you can beat my head in or back-shoot me. But you'd be a fool to try. I didn't come here without a hole card.'

Larson nodded sombrely – 'He wouldn't come without a hole card, Ray. Not this one.'

Glory's smile was ghastly.

'You think you can make me back up to that kind of crap?' he demanded. 'Why, you cheap, two-bit son-of-a-bitch, I'm goin' to show you what kind of trash you are.'

'How?'

'Phil here is going to take you out and throw you to my wolves.'

Larson looked just the smallest bit startled. But he also knew an order when he heard it. Blade could see the resolution forming in his hard eyes. It was Larson's intention to make the fastest draw he ever made in his life. But he never made it.

Blade turned on him suddenly and said: 'Don't do it, Larson. You move your left hand and you're dead. Now, let me see both your hands.'

Larson went very still for a moment. His face looked as if it had been hacked out of ice. He didn't look at Glory. His eyes never left Blade's face. If there was any weakness there, he would see it. He had been looking for the weakness in men's faces all his life. Mostly he found it. Now he found none. This man had every confidence that he was faster and better than the great Phil Larson.

'I suppose,' he said with monumental calm, 'you're going to tell me you have a gun under the table.'

'That's what I'm telling you.'

Larson cleared his throat and the small sound was like thunder in the quiet room.

'Let me see it,' he said.

Blade pushed his chair back and stood up. His right hand was empty. The two men faced each other across the table. At the head of the table, Glory sat crouched, his eyes avid. He waited to see a man killed and that man must be Blade.

Blade said: 'As you see, it was in its scabbard. It didn't need to be anywhere else. Now you draw, Larson, if that's what you want.'

The older man licked his dry lips. His face was grey. Sooner or later, he had to meet up with one of the Blades of this world. He knew now it was sooner than later.

Blade said: 'You'll always ask yourself who was the faster, you or me. As the years pass you'll convince yourself you were the faster. So I'll show you.'

Glory whispered urgently: 'Kill him, Phil.'

Larson said: 'You want him dead, Ray. You do it.'

Blade's right hand moved. There was no more than a whisper of sound as the big Colt came out of oiled leather.

'Unbuckle your belt,' Blade said, 'and let it drop.'

Larson sighed softly and did as he was ordered. The gun and the belt hit the floor with a dull sound. The old gunman sat there looking drained. This had never happened to him before. Blade knew a little pity for him.

He said: 'Walk ahead of me, both of you. I guess I'll ride now. This is your last chance to make a deal, Glory.'

'Go to hell,' Glory said.

They walked ahead of him.

In the hall, they met June Howard. She smiled bewitchingly at Blade as he passed her. She said: 'Why, Mr Glory, you don't look as in command of the situation as usual.'

Blade tipped his hat to her and said: 'I'll bid you good day, Miss June.'

She pursed up her lips in a kiss to him. She looked good enough to eat as she did so.

When they reached the gallery, Blade saw that his horse was gone. The men stood in a half-circle, watching him. Several of them had guns in their hands. Blade went close up behind Glory and thrust the muzzle of the Colt into his neck. The man shrank under the touch of the small circle of steel.

'Call off your wolves, Glory,' Blade said.

Glory swallowed a couple of times, then valiantly tried to act tough in front of his men.

'This is a Mexican standoff, Blade,' he said. 'Put down your gun or it could go bad for you.'

Blade laughed – 'They put down their guns or it could be pretty damn bad for *you*, Glory. Half Texas won't do you much good with a bullet through your neck.'

Larson said: 'Call it a day, Ray. What you can't do today you can do tomorrow.'

One of the men called out: 'Throw down your iron, Blade, or I make smoke.'

A small spurt of dust appeared in the yard to one side of the men. A couple of them jumped as the flat slam of Prescott's Winchester drifted across the land.

Blade said: 'There's Santiago men up there in the brush and a couple between here and the creek.'

One of the men said: 'I told you he wasn't fool enough to come in here single-handed.'

Larson said with authority: 'Quit this damn foolery, men. Put up your guns.'

'Better still,' said Blade, 'throw 'em on the ground.'

'Go ahead,' Larson told them. 'Nobody's blamin' you. You can't win 'em all.'

They placed their guns on the ground and backed up. Blade pushed Glory down off the gallery and manœuvred him between himself and the men. Then he eased across the yard to a sorrel horse tied to a corral rail. He could see the men restraining themselves with difficulty from jumping for their guns.

He said: 'How about the deal, Glory?'

The man screwed his head around and glared into Blade's eyes.

'I'll hang you, Blade,' he said, choking on the words. 'I'll hang you.'

Blade's left hand freed the horse's tied line. He stepped carefully into the saddle and the horse whirled. A man jumped for the guns on the ground. Blade drove a shot an inch in front of him and the man jumped back. Glory tried to get clear of the horse, but its rump caught him and sent him flying. Blade yelled to the horse and kicked it with his spurless heels. The animal jumped forward and ran. The last thing that Blade heard was Glory's yell of pure fury.

When he glanced back, every man there had a gun in his hand and was firing. Larson remained where he was on the gallery, watching him go. As the sorrel breasted the ridge, Blade looked back again and saw the men catching up their horses in the corral. Old True Prescott was in the saddle ready by the time Blade reached him. The old man gave a wild rebel yell as he turned his horse alongside him. Side by side, they raced away.

As they went, the old man shouted: 'Damned if it ain't like old times. Your style sure do suit me, Joe.'

12

When they reached Esmeralda's house, the dun horse had come home and everybody there seemed to think that Blade must be dead. No, he said, he wasn't dead, just dead tired. He and Prescott ate one of Mrs Díaz's meals and related what they had been doing. Esmeralda seemed momentarily defeated on hearing that Glory and Howard had thrown in together, but Blade would have none of it. They knew their enemies now. They knew that both men spelled the same danger to Santiago.

So what could they do now? the girl demanded.

'Burn Glory's place,' said Blade.

All who heard him were aghast. They knew that it made sense to take the war to the enemy – when the enemy was weak. But how could they muster enough men to attack the Glory headquarters? Would men be willing to risk their lives in an open raid? Glory had an army on his payroll. A shortage of men was not their problem, Esmeralda said – twenty or so more had come in asking for work. The word was getting around. But these men were labourers, not fighting men.

Blade said: 'To wipe Glory out we need one man. Or, at most, two.'

Old Prescott slapped the table with the flat of his hand so that the cups and plates jumped.

'That's me an' Joe,' he said.

'Maybe it is, at that, old-timer,' Blade said.

'We make a dang good team does me an' Joe,' True avowed.

'No,' said Esmeralda in the voice of a woman accustomed to

giving orders to men and having them obeyed. 'Most definitely no. And that is final.'

'We shall want some dynamite, Joe,' Prescott said. 'Where can we lay our hands on some dynamite?'

'Did you hear me, Trueman,' Esmeralda demanded, 'or are you deaf?'

'Leave this to us men, honey,' said old True. 'Don't you worry your pretty head about a thing.'

The night was black as pitch. Old True Prescott was coughing his head off as he led the way (unerringly again, Blade hoped) through the fathomless night.

'Quit that fool coughing, True,' Blade called softly, 'or you're liable to go sky high and come down in a fine red rain with all that damn dynamite you're carrying.'

The old man snapped back: 'It's this damn bromkittis a feller gits from ridin' damp nights for unappreciative owners.'

As if he had made a prophecy, it began to rain. True cursed with the efficiency of long years of practice, but Blade was pleased enough. Nobody was going around willingly on a wet night.

Gradually, the rain increased until they were leaning into the full drive of it, huddled in their oilskins. The horses wanted to turn away from it and the two men were constantly forcing them to keep going in line ahead. For hour after hour, it seemed they listened to the continuous sound of the rain as it drummed on the oiled cloth. That tune was orchestrated by the soft rain-hushed jingle of the bridle-chains, the creak of leather and the steady plod-plod of their horses' feet.

It seemed an age before the old man halted and Blade's horse swerved to avoid the animal in front. Almost alongside, True said: 'I ain't too sure, Joe, but I reckon we're pretty close.'

They stepped down from their saddles. The horses hung

their heads under the onslaught of the rain. The old man chuckled.

'This'll sure fill the ditches,' he said.

'Where do you reckon the house is from here?' Blade asked.

The old man hesitated a moment. Then he stabbed a gnarled forefinger at the dark.

'Yonder,' he said. 'Don't fret, I'll take you in real close.'

They tied their horses and took the saddlebags off the saddles. Blade reckoned this was about the craziest thing he had done in his life and that was saying something. In the past, he had taken risks for a living or a fat profit. There was no profit in this. He must be getting quixotic in his old age.

True must have read his thoughts: 'You know we're as crazy as coots doin' this. All right for a young feller like you, but I ought to know better.'

'If there were coots as crazy as this,' Blade said, 'they'd lock 'em up.'

'Like I said, boy, you got style,' True said. 'All right, let's go.' He took a pace down off the ridge and lost his footing on the rain-wet surface. With a wild squeal of alarm, he disappeared from sight.

Blade held his breath. The sound of the old man going down the side of the ridge lasted for an awfully long time. Then there came the crash of damp brush and the old man's almost hysterical curses. Blade started down the steep grade with great care.

When he reached the bottom, True was picking himself out of the brush.

'I lost the goddam dynamite some goddam place,' he said.

They searched around for the dynamite. Blade found it about a dozen yards off. He said: 'True, I guess you have a certain style of your own.' The old man laughed, then Blade laughed and they laughed so much they had to cling to each other to stop themselves slipping over in the mud.

Finally, True said: 'Son, I don't reckon we're approachin'

the business in hand with due seriousness.' And that started them laughing some more.

'You gotta admit,' said True as they shouldered their way through the driving rain, 'that kinda showed we got luck. Hell, I could of blowed us sky high with that dynamite.'

Twenty minutes later, the old man halted abruptly. He had walked into a corral fence.

'This is it, Joe,' he said. 'I can see the light from the bunk-house yonder.'

They tramped on until they reached the door of the bunk-house. They had no sooner reached it than they were startled to see the door open. All they could see were the hat and slicker of a man about to step out into the rain. True, who was in the lead, said cordially: 'Howdy.'

'Howdy.' said the man. 'Who is this?' True hit him with his gun barrel. As he collapsed on the ground, the old man stepped over him into the building and said: 'Outa your bunks, you sonsabitches, or we blow you to smithereens where you lie. It ain't no goddam no-never-mind to us'ns which way you want it.'

Blade walked into the close air of the bunkhouse and saw the astonished eyes of the men as they sat up in their bunks. One or two faces he recognised from his last visit. He brought his own gun from under his slicker and barked: 'Move it.'

There was not a word spoken. Men climbed from their bunks, automatically hauling their boots on. One or two reached for their slickers, but Blade would have none of that. In their longjohns, they moved sheepishly towards the door. True backed away ahead of them, keeping them covered with his gun. He pointed to the unconscious man on the ground – 'Haul that fallen hero out with you.'

When they were huddled in the rain outside the building, Blade said: 'The place is surrounded. We start dynamiting straight off. Leg it up to the big house and tell Glory to get the folks out because we're going to blow it to hell.'

The men hesitated. Who had the grit to take a message like that to Glory? True let go a couple of shots and that started them running. By the time they were halfway to the house, Blade had lobbed the first stick of dynamite through the doorway of the bunkhouse. By the time the men reached the big house, the bunkhouse went up with a roar. The roof seemed to lift off and the walls to lean out and fall. Blade, who had run almost to the corral, was nearly thrown from his feet. Old True gave a wild yell of triumph and shouted: 'Let 'er rip. Cheyenne, here I come.'

What was left of the bunkhouse was burning. The flames lit up the next building that looked like a storehouse. True knocked in a window and dropped a stick of dynamite inside with its fuse buzzing. His running was not of the best and the blast from the explosion knocked him from his feet into the mud. He received the upset with the greatest delight.

'I ain't had so much fun in years,' he howled, staggering to his feet.

'Work your way around to the rear of the house,' Blade said.

They both hunched their way through the rain into the darkness.

Raymond Glory had been working on June Howard all evening. He had tried everything he knew – and he reckoned his knowledge was considerable. They had dined by candlelight on the best cuisine the cook was capable of and now Glory plied June with his best brandy. If this combination wouldn't soften up a woman, he didn't know what would. Officially, it was a dinner to celebrate the union of the two powerful men.

Howard sat flushed with wine at Glory's right hand. His usually pale pink cheeks carried bright red patches. His eyes glistened in the soft light.

Narcissa sat to the right of her husband, looking like a marble statue. She had drunk more than enough wine, but she seemed immune to it. She had scarcely spoken a word the whole evening. Opposite her, Chard watched the proceedings with cold eyes.

June, to Glory's left, looked sulky. She kept her eyes away from Glory who, by this time, was starting to shows signs that he had drunk too much. Phil Larson sat beyond Narcissa and took part in the evening with about as much enthusiasm as Chard displayed.

Glory was saying: 'We could start a new dynasty, Howard. Hey, there's an idea. How about me an' Miss June? Ain't that a dandy idea, now? Join our two empires together.'

June looked at her father and was horrified to see that he received the remark with what passed for him as pleasure.

'Time enough to think about that kind of thing,' he said. 'But let's say that I see no real reason why I should look upon such a suggestion with disfavour.'

Glory swung on June – 'You hear that, young lady? Your papa don't think it such a bad idea.'

Narcissa's attention was taken by a small movement on the far side of the table and, turning her eyes from Glory she was surprised to see a look of uncontrollable fury on Chard's face. She knew then the grey man's secret.

So that's the way the wind blows, she thought.

Glory took hold of June's hand as it lay on the table and raised it to his lips.

Chard leapt to his feet and ground out: 'This has gone far enough, Mr Howard. You should be ashamed.'

Howard looked up in owlish surprise.

But the situation had no opportunity to develop further than that. As Glory shouted: 'Siddown an' shut up, Chard,' there came the dull boom of an explosion. The house shook.

Now they were all on their feet.

'What the hell was that?' Glory demanded.

Larson moved. And he moved fast. Wrenching the door open, he ran down the hall and out on to the gallery. They all followed him. From the direction of the bunkhouse they heard wild shouts. Chard yelled: 'Stay inside, ladies,' but they ignored him.

From the gallery, they saw flickering flames from the burning bunkhouse. By its light, they could see the pale figures of men running.

'My God,' Howard cried in horror, 'they are unclothed. Get the ladies inside.'

As he spoke, there came a second explosion and its force nearly flung them from their feet. One or two of the running figures fell over in the mud of the yard.

A man reached the gallery and bellowed at Glory: 'They're goin' to blow up the house, Mr Glory.'

Larson jumped into the yard, gun in hand, shouting: 'Where're they at?'

'There's a dozen of 'em, Phil,' somebody told him. 'They got the place surrounded.'

It sounded as though Glory were in some sort of frenzy. He did a kind of enraged dance up and down the gallery in front of the door, bellowing: 'Nobody can blow up *my* house. Larson, do somethin', you goddam fool.' He ran back into the house, bawling for somebody to give him a gun.

'Get back into the house,' Howard ordered the ladies.

'Hardly a sensible suggestion,' said Chard, 'when we've just been told the house is about to be blown up.'

Howard looked at Chard in amazement. He saw that Chard had his coat off and had placed it around June's shoulders.

'This way, Miss June,' he said. 'This way, Mrs Howard.'

Larson was firing into the darkness. There came a couple of shots in reply and glass crashed as windows collapsed in one of the rooms.

One of the men yelled: 'It's that goddam Blade.'

Chard was saying to the girls as he hurried them through the mud away from the house: 'It's all right, ladies, you have nothing to fear. It's only Mr Blade.' He guided them towards the burning buildings. 'The fire over here will keep you warm and Mr Blade will be able to see you and will know not to shoot in your direction.'

Narcissa said: 'You seem very calm, Mr Chard.'

'Thank you, ma'am,' he said.

The Chinese cook came howling through the hall, across the gallery and into the yard, announcing to the world that there were men shooting at the rear of the house and telling him that they intended to blow it up. The men in their longjohns didn't know which way to go. Mainly, they felt more stupid than scared.

Then Glory came roaring out of the house with his arms full of guns. He started handing them out to the men, shouting at them to kill the bastards.

'What with?' one of the men asked. 'We don't have any ammunition.'

At this point, Glory appeared to break into tears. The next second, there was a loud explosion from the rear of the house and he yelled: 'My house, my house.'

After that, there came three more explosions in quick succession and the building seemed to start caving in. But the men didn't see much of the spectacle, for they were running for their lives. When they did haul up and turn for a good look, the timber structure was burning quite brightly.

In the middle of the yard, looking less effectual than any other time of his life, Glory shook his fist and bellowed at the top of his voice: 'I'll hang you for this, Blade.'

June Howard called to him: 'You should learn to listen, Mr Glory. Joe Blade told you he'd burn your house down if you didn't agree to his terms. You have only yourself to blame.'

'Yes, indeedy,' said Chard. 'How true.'

Howard heard that. He stamped up to his man of business and said: 'I heard that, Chard. What in heaven's name has gotten into you, man? Have you taken leave of your senses?'

'No, sir,' said Chard stoutly, 'just come to 'em. I think your offering a fine girl like Miss June to that whisky-swilling Texas hog is just about the limit.'

Howard gave a fair imitation of Raymond Glory. He positively danced.

'One more word out of you, Chard,' he said, 'and you're fired.'

'With respect, Mr Howard,' said Chard, 'you may go to hell. Ladies, I suggest that I escort you to Laredo.'

Narcissa said: 'An excellent idea, Mr Chard.'

The two ladies started forward, each holding one of Chard's arms.

'Narcissa, June, come back here this instant,' said Howard.

He watched them walk away from him in the teeming rain. He stood there wondering how so powerful a man could feel so helpless. He wondered if throwing his lot in with Raymond Glory had anything to do with it. He had a headache and he did not feel very well. He decided that he was going to make somebody suffer for all this. Preferably Joe Blade. But right now there didn't seem much chance of that.

13

Peace fell over Santiago. But it was an uneasy peace and men moved about their work with caution. Their eyes went perpetually to the ridge, watchful for the distant silhouettes of riders. They stayed together in bunches, and that tended to slow their work. However, Blade insisted that no man wandered off from his crew alone. Except for the scouts. All the time, at all hours, he had scouts on the look-out. He was determined that Santiago would suffer no more surprise attacks or burning down of houses.

Glory and Howard certainly stayed quiet for a long while. Some of the Santiago folk said that even big men like these two knew when they were licked. But the more sophisticated ones like Harry Simpson reckoned the two magnates were biding their time. Neither backed losers, and any deal they had in their hands had to be a winner. Their pride excluded anything less. They had been hit hard, it was admitted, but their silence meant they were consolidating and reorganising their tactics.

Blade was also of this opinion. Several times during the next month, he ventured, when he could spare the time from work, on to Glory land and spied it out, going carefully with a Winchester in his hand. He saw the efforts Glory was making to rebuild his destroyed home. Maybe he was waiting to make his try against Santiago until he had a strong fortress built. This time he was building with adobe and there was an army of Mexican workers swarming like ants over the building site, brought out from Laredo in carts and wagons. Cattle were slaughtered and roasted whole over great fires. Glory didn't do things on a small scale, not ever. It was a wonder the wages he was offering did not draw men away from Santiago, but they did not.

When Blade inquired the possible reason for this of Garcia, the Mexican replied: '*Patrón*, here on Santiago, the people know they have a future. You will see, there will be a village here. Already men are bringing out their women and children.'

As the days passed, whole families drove out from town to see the work in progress. They made a two-day trip of it, sleeping out under the stars, for the rain had stopped as suddenly as it had come. The creeks were full and some of the ditches already had water in them. Blade told Esmeralda that he had a fruit farmer coming out from Florida to advise them. Esmeralda herself seemed to work from dawn to dusk. She slaughtered Santiago cattle and fed the visitors in the old style as her father had. She was like a new woman, moving graciously and with charm among the Laredo folk. Blade was pleased by the presence of the sightseers for more than one reason, but mainly because nobody was going to raid Santiago with so many eyewitnesses.

Blade was also amused by the fact that Harry Simpson was never too far from Esmeralda's side. The man seemed to have a fresh look to him. The flabby pallor had gone from his face, and his body was hardening from the work he was putting in on the ditches. All the men worked while they could see and fell into their blankets exhausted after dark. The wagon trains moved back and forth from Laredo with equipment and supplies, the armed guards sitting up beside the drivers. They brought out ploughs and soon the yokes of oxen were straining the plough blades through the virgin soil.

The Florida fruit man bounced into Laredo on a noon coach and then horsebacked out to Santiago to survey the land.

He threw up his hands and declared with the certainty of the expert that no fruit would grow here. 'My God,' he declared, 'you could grow nothing here, not even good grass.'

So they took him horsebacking over the hills and stood guard with their rifles while he took a look at the fruit trees in the irrigated valley and told him that the soil down there was the same as Santiago and he said: 'Impossible.' Later, he gave signs of eating his words.

'Everybody has to be wrong once in a while,' he said and Blade allowed him just that one mistake.

'You grow fruit in Santiago,' he said, 'and you'll go back to Florida with silver in your pockets. You fail and I'll drop you in the Rio Grande.'

And all this time, the law did nothing. Neither the local law, such as it was, nor the Rangers. So Blade concluded that McNally at least was going to sit on the sidelines and see how things went. He wasn't going to fall foul of a man as big as Glory if he could help it, and he knew Blade.

Rumour came out to Santiago from town that there was heavy betting that Glory would have Blade dead before the end of the year. And the betting claimed that Phil Larson would do the killing. Larson, it was said, was smarting under the defeat he had suffered at Blade's hands at Glory's place. How the tale had got out, Blade never knew. But gossip had a way of being right and Blade watched his back even in open country. Old True Prescott heard the talk and would never allow Blade to ride out without him.

'Even an old fool like me,' he said, 'can squeeze a trigger. That don't call for too much energy and strength.'

Blade had his own ideas on what to expect. It seemed logical to him that, as Jim Flaherty had been killed by a Mexican and Harry Simpson's office had been burned down by Mexicans, the attack on him would come from a man or men in the same guise. He saw also that it was important to his cause which way the local law would jump – on the side of

Santiago or that of the Howard-Glory faction. He therefore decided to take the bull by the horns and rode into Laredo to have a word with Captain McNally of the Texas Rangers.

By this time, the several weeks of uninterrupted work had lulled many of the Santiago people into a false sense of security. Some men were starting to say that even a big man like Raymond Glory had learned better than to meddle with Santiago. But neither Blade nor old True Prescott were fooled. Even as they trotted their horses down the Laredo road, True said to Blade: 'If Glory don't have this road watched, Joe, I'm a Dutchman. By the time we hit town, Ray Glory will have a trap baited. Bank on it.'

'I'm not arguing,' Blade said. 'You could be right.'

He wondered if Howard was back in town and whether he would get to see either June or Narcissa Howard.

On the surface, Laredo seemed much as usual – noisy, colourful, men sleeping in the sun and waiting for tomorrow, or rushing in Anglo manner to make another buck before tomorrow came. The hawkers sang their wares shrilly on the streets, the stallholders were there in the markets with their baskets of red, yellow and green peppers, cockerels squawked as they swung by their heels in brown hands, bright eyes and teeth flashed in Mexican faces, and the rich pungent Mexican smell that Blade loved pervaded the whole scene. Their horses clip-clopped their way past the burned out ruins of Simpson's office. Heads turned idly to watch the two horsemen pass. Blade looked up as they went by the hotel and he raised a hand in greeting as Narcissa Howard looked out from a window. He turned his head to watch her, savouring her smile.

As they neared the Ranger headquarters, True said: 'I got a feelin' in my bones, Joe. There's real trouble here today.'

They halted in front of the office and swung down from their horses. As they tied their animals, Blade said: 'This shouldn't take long, True.'

The old man said: 'I'll hang around.' He meant that he

would watch the street. Plainly, he didn't think it was safe for him and Blade, not even with the Rangers so close.

Blade found the building almost deserted. Captain McNally was in the office smoking a stogie.

Blade said: 'Where's everybody today?'

'Chasin' bandidos along the river,' the captain told him. 'What can I do for you, Joe?'

Blade told him.

Outside, squatting on his heels in the shade of the sidewalk cover, True Prescott eyed the street. Three riders loped into town from the north-east and the old man stiffened instantly at the sight of them. The man in the lead on the long-legged sorrel was Phil Larson. The second man was Lee Tolliver. The third man True saw was Chuck Kiver, a known gunhand. Not one of them turned his head to look at True, but he knew they had not failed to see him. Larson had eyes like a hawk.

True built himself a smoke. It was down to a discarded butt by the time Blade came out of the office.

'Well?' True asked.

'McNally's still sitting on the fence,' Blade told him. 'Except if there's any gunplay in town. In which case, he arrests everybody in sight.'

'Rangers,' said True, 'just ain't what they was in my day. Every damn thing has gone to hell.' Blade untied his horse. 'Hold hard now – Larson just rode into town with Tolliver and Kiver. And it ain't no coincidence.'

Blade mounted and the old man followed suit.

Blade said: 'I never heard of Larson backshooting a man.'

'Backshoot, frontshoot,' snapped the old man. 'Where the hell's the difference? Either way you can be plumb dead. There's a heap at stake and Larson has to be a lowdown son-off-a-bitch or he wouldn't of hired on with a no-good bastard like Glory. So my vote says we hightail it out of town and don't mooch around pickin' daisies an' the like.'

Blade settled his gun scabbard more comfortably and unlatched the safety thong.

They had not gone a block through town when Blade saw Narcissa Howard on the sidewalk beckoning to him. He turned his horse in her direction and True followed with the whispered words: 'It could be a trap, Joe.' But Blade was not willing to believe that. He was aware that the old man had turned his horse to face the street. His own eyes flicked upward involuntarily in search of a half-concealed gunman. He saw nothing suspicious.

Narcissa's face was anxious.

'Blade,' she said, 'they plan to kill you in town today.'

'You're taking a risk, Mrs Howard,' he said. 'Anybody can see you here.'

'I know. But June and I could not bear to see you shot down,' she told him. 'There's been enough bloodshed already.'

'It'll be all right,' he said. 'True spotted Larson and his two men.'

'It won't be Larson,' she said. 'I heard my husband and Raymond Glory talking. They'll use Mexicans, as usual.'

So, Blade thought, *Larson is merely here to observe and report back.*

'We're in debt to you, Narcissa,' he said, using her given name for the first time. 'I won't forget.'

He smiled. She gave him a wavering, frightened smile back. He reckoned it had cost her a lot to come out here on to the street to warn him, probably knowing that her husband was watching her.

'Joe,' she said as he started to wheel his horse away from her, 'please don't get yourself killed.'

He smiled and said: 'Nothing was further from my thoughts.' She lifted a hand to him.

The next moment, Blade and the old man were trotting their horses down the street.

'Mrs Howard told me,' Blade said, 'they plan to have Mexicans kill us.'

'Izzatso?' was the only comment the old man made.

They travelled another hundred yards and there, suddenly, was Phil Larson sitting his horse quietly at the side of the street.

'Larson,' said True dramatically out of the side of his mouth.

'I see him.'

Blade did not alter the pace of his horse. As they came opposite Larson, Blade's eyes and those of the veteran gunman met. Larson lifted a hand in mute salutation and Blade responded.

'Of all the goddam cool nerve,' True muttered.

Within minutes, they were on the edge of town. They lifted their horses to a lope and True said: 'That was kind of a let down, Joe. I was all primed for the shindig.'

Blade spied dust ahead of them on the road and said: 'I think you just spoke too soon, True.'

He turned in his saddle and saw riders come out of town behind them. He sighed softly. He knew the enemy had laid the simplest and best trap of all. They planned to kill him and True out on the open road away from the town where there would be eyewitnesses to the killing.

The old man cackled jubilantly – 'The odds ain't so bad, Joe. Two up front an' two behind.' He cocked his head in thought as they both reined in their mouths, then said: 'Oliver Loving taught me a little thing out on the Staked Plain against the Comanch'. We was in a fix kinda like this, two bunches comin' at us back an' front. We run our horses to get their second wind. Then we stopped real quick and shot their asses off a mite. That stopped 'em awhile. Who likes havin' his ass shot off? Then we hightailed it outa there. Whatya think, huh? It ain't much, but I don't have nothin' more to offer right this minute.'

Blade smiled – 'Sounds fine. We'll cut east and make 'em think we're headed for open country.'

With that, he turned his horse off the road and sent it at a high lope towards the blue and distant line of the hills. He heard True yelp to his horse and come after him. When he glanced back, he saw, as he expected, that all four horsemen had left the road and were now angling in on him and True, pushing their horses to the limit of their speed.

True shouted: 'Them bastards is well mounted, boy, an' no mistake.'

When Blade next looked back, he saw that the pursuers were gaining on them steadily. They ran on for another mile and the two Santiago horses were well into their strides. They came to a slight dip in the plain and True yelled: 'Here, Joe.'

They heaved their mounts to a halt, leapt from their saddles, tore their Winchesters from the saddle-boots and threw themselves down. As soon as they hit dirt, they were firing, for the riders were uncomfortably close. As soon as they started firing, the foremost rider seemed to fade away before them. Horse and rider went down under their lead and stayed still. The other three riders divided on either side of them and rode past them, blazing away from the saddle. Blade had never seen such a high standard of shooting from the backs of speeding horses. He glanced at True and realised that the old man was taken aback by the performance.

'Hell,' he exclaimed, 'they flanked us.' He rose to one knee and fired at the backs of the riders. Blade could not see too well. There was a lot of dust about, most of it kicked up by their riderless horses which had taken alarm and were trying to run in spite of their dragging lines. True started cursing the animals.

The riders turned, one of them rearing his horse and whirling it on a space that could have been covered by a lady's pocket handkerchief. When the horse came down, its legs crumpled under it like paper. The rider was pitched helplessly from the saddle. True and Blade fired together, snapping shots at the man. Then the other two were riding down on them hard, firing as they came.

To Blade, it seemed that the ground was torn up on either side of him by rifle fire. The air around him seemed to be full of flying lead. Suddenly, a horse and rider were right on top of him, a great black shape between him and the blinding azure of the sky. He flung himself clear, firing at a range of no more than a dozen feet. The rider was flung violently over the neck of his racing horse, clung there for a moment and then fell to the ground. The horse ran on towards the Laredo road.

True fired a shot at the other rider as he passed and said in quiet disgust: 'Missed.'

Blade said: 'I reckon that's enough for one day.'

True did not reply. He was sitting on the ground with his chin on his chest. Suddenly alarmed, Blade said: 'True.'

The old man lifted his head and smiled. Blade saw the blood on his thin chest. True said: 'I'm cashin' in, son. Best way to go. The rheumatiz was gettin' somethin' terrible.'

He laid himself down full-length on the ground. When Blade knelt beside him, True said: 'Like I said – you got style, Joe.'

Blade said: 'I'll get you into town to a doctor, True.'

'Like hell you do,' True snapped feebly. 'You fork your hay-burner an' go git that Mex. Give him to the Rangers.'

He closed his eyes and died.

Blade stood up. He had had very few partners in his professional career. There had never been a better one than this old man. He looked around for the surviving rider and saw him a couple of hundred yards away, sitting on his horse and watching him.

Softly, Blade said: 'You're for the Rangers, *chico*, just like True said.'

He walked to his horse and caught it. Putting the Winchester away, he swung into the saddle. The other rider had not moved. Blade lifted the horse to a trot. The man spurred his horse and turned it, heading for Laredo.

Blade thought: *You can cross the border, you can ride all the way to Mexico City, but you won't shake me.*

14

That morning, the citizens of Laredo no sooner recovered themselves from the insane charge of the Mexican rider through their streets, than the quiet of the town was again broken by the insane charge of the grey-haired gringo. Men, women, children, dogs and chickens scattered before Blade's galloping horse with the same alacrity with which they had escaped the Mexican's. And, as with the Mexican, the dogs closed in behind him, snapping and snarling bravely at the horse's retreating heels.

Captain McNally of the Rangers, returning to his office after being summoned from it by the sound of the Mexican's passage, turned to see Blade storming down the street. McNally's Ranger nose smelled trouble.

'Hold up,' he bellowed as Blade came abreast of him, but Blade went on by without so much as a glance at him. All that McNally could do was hope fervently that Blade would catch the Mexican below the Border and not on the United States side.

Blade lost ground going through town. Not only was the Mexican mounted on a superior horse, but he showed less concern than Blade for the safety of the people on the streets. Anger aroused by the pursued among the people was centred on the pursuer. Men shook their fists at him and women screamed abuse. As Blade approached the frontier post on the American side, he thought his cause was lost, for a man wearing the badge of the Texas Rangers barred his way with outstretched arms. Not willing to run down a wearer of that badge nor to invite an official bullet in his back as he galloped into Mexico, Blade reined in his horse.

'What's the all-fired hurry, mister?' the tall Ranger inquired.

Blade said: 'That son-of-a-bitch just killed my partner.'

The man looked a little startled. 'He did? Hell, I know him – that's Pepe Suarez. He's back an' forth all the time.'

Blade said: 'If you get out of my road, he won't be back and forth much longer.'

The Ranger stepped aside briskly, saying: 'Be my guest.'

Blade thanked him and kicked his horse into a run. Now was the most urgent need for speed, for, at that time, there was no bridge at Laredo and the width of the Rio Grande could only be crossed by ferries, propelled by poles, as one traveller put it 'at Mexican speed'. As Blade reached the water's edge, the flat-boat which served as a ferry was already thirty or forty feet on its way across the great river. At the rear of the ferry stood Pepe Suarez, watching Blade's frustration with a broad and delighted smile.

It was that smile that did it. Maybe if that happy Mexican had kept his lips closed over those bright teeth, Blade would have said: 'To hell with it' and gone back the way he had come. However, Blade put his horse at the water and prayed that he had a good swimming horse. He certainly had no idea of whether he had or not, for he had never put the animal to anything deeper than a shallow creek.

As luck would have it, the game animal did not hesitate, but breasted the wide expanse of the river with a will. Blade slipped from its back and grabbed it by its tail so that it could swim with the greatest freedom.

When he looked at the man in the stern of the ferry, he saw that he was no longer smiling so happily. In fact, the man was apparently yelling to the men wielding the poles, urging them to move the clumsy craft at a faster pace. To Blade's surprise, he saw that his gallant horse was actually gaining slightly on the ferry.

Even so, the ferry reached Mexican soil first and Blade, while still in the water, saw the man Suarez get ashore and go spurring up to the Mexican border post. He saw the man pointing back at him and did not doubt that the Mexican guards were being warned of an undesirable *gringo* who was about to come ashore. As soon as Blade reached the land, he swung dripping with Rio Grande water into a wet saddle and thundered up to the frontier post. He was met by a couple of rifles aimed at his chest and stopped to watch his quarry disappear rapidly from sight.

A Mexican officer cried: '*Alto*' with some drama and held up his hand. 'You will dismount, señor.'

Blade showed mild surprise – 'There is something wrong, *capitán*?' His excellent Spanish shook them a little.

The officer's voice softened somewhat – 'I believe you are in pursuit of a Mexican citizen, señor.'

'I am in pursuit of a murderer.'

'I regret that it is not permitted for you to go any further.'

Blade knew that nothing could be gained by argument, only time lost. He flicked his horse sharply with his quirt and jumped it sideways. It barged against one of the *rurales* holding a rifle and knocked him from his feet, then it moved forward in two jumps and struck a second man. The officer jumped back, struggling to unfasten the catch of his revolver holster. Blade's horse got its legs under it and ran. He heard the officer shouting for him to halt or they would shoot, but his only response was to lie along the neck of his horse and to use the quirt. A bullet knocked up the dirt ahead of him, another shot passed close by his right ear.

The officer yelled: 'To horse, men. Catch that man.'

Blade thundered on into Mexico.

The way men tell it, neither hide nor hair was seen of Joe Blade then or for several days. In that time, the Rangers had back-tracked him to the plain north-east of town and found the bodies of True Prescott and the Mexicans. Captain McNally was heard to say that he would like nothing better than a few minutes' conversation with one Joseph Blade, at the end of which he did not doubt that he would fasten a pair of handcuffs on his wrists. Not that he really thought he would see Joe Blade again. Pepe Suarez had a good many very tough friends below the Border and they would no doubt settle Blade's hash.

However, he was surprised one evening, several days later when, on hearing horses halted in the street outside his office, he walked out to see the same Blade with a Mexican. The Mexican was tied securely to his own saddle. The worthy captain was about to say: 'You are under arrest,' but he never had the chance, for Blade said: 'This is Pepe Suarez, who maybe you heard about already, captain. I'm charging him with the murder of Jim Flaherty. If you question him efficiently, you will find that he conspired with Raymond Glory to murder *me*.'

'Is that so?' said McNally, who was not a man to believe all he heard. 'Get down, the pair of you, and let's talk about it.'

The good people of Laredo, who were always more interested in anybody else's business rather than their own, were interested to see that Blade entered the Ranger building with the captain and the prisoner. There was some talk between the three of them, the upshot of which McNally decided that the Mexican, Pepe Suarez, was indeed rightly to be accused of murder. So he promptly escorted him to jail and incarcerated him therein. McNally was seen to spend some time on the street talking amiably enough with Joe Blade.

McNally's final words were: 'Blade, I don't know what the hell is going on around here, but, as sure as God made little apples, something is.'

Blade asked: 'Do you know if Glory is at the bottom of it?'

'I guess he is.'

'Are you big enough to go against him?'

'Depends on the circumstances, but I ain't a damn fool if that's what you mean.'

Dark had fallen by now. Blade wished him good night and headed down the street with the two horses, planning to leave them at the livery and ride out on a fresh one to the Santiago grant. Before he could reach the livery, however, he was stopped by Chard who had been watching the street from the hotel window. The man appeared to be in a very distressed state and Blade soon learned why.

'The two Howard ladies have been taken, Blade,' he said.

'What?' Blade cried. 'Who in God's name would do a thing like that?'

Chard told him: 'Mr Howard is convinced that you're the guilty party. He thinks that, in your desperation to frighten him off Santiago, you have resorted to kidnapping.'

'He must be out of his mind. Chard, you don't believe this, do you?'

'No, I don't,' Chard replied, 'but that hasn't prevented Mr Howard from recruiting an army of riffraff to go against Santiago.'

This information filled Blade with a kind of horror.

'Is there any way we can stop him?' he demanded. 'How far has he gone with this crazy idea?'

'He's still here in town,' Chard said. 'His deadline is tomorrow. He has sent a letter in reply to Esmeralda Santiago's, telling her that if she doesn't surrender the two ladies by noon, he will wipe the place out.'

'A letter from Esmeralda? Telling Howard she holds June and Narcissa? I don't believe it.'

'Well, Howard certainly believes it. I must get back now. There'll be hell to pay if he sees me talking to you.'

He never did get back, for, as chance would have it, at that moment a horseman galloped down the street, almost running them down in the uncertain evening light.

The rider was Harry Simpson.

'Harry,' Blade called.

The rider reined and jumped from the saddle.

'Where've you been?' Harry demanded. 'All hell's broken loose.'

'What happened?' Blade asked.

'Esmeralda's been taken.'

'This is too goddam ridiculous,' Blade said in a kind of despair.

Chard said: 'It don't make any kind of sense.'

'I don't care what kind of sense it makes,' Harry snapped. 'It's the goddam truth. Joe, I'm out of my mind with worry.'

Blade told him what Chard had told him. Harry looked from one to the other in utter amazement.

'Joe,' Harry said at last, 'are you thinking what I'm thinking?'

'You bet your sweet life I am,' said Blade.

Chard demanded: 'What's that?'

'Glory has the three women. He must have gone loco.'

'What're you going to do?'

'First, I see Howard.'

The three of them headed for the hotel. A flustered manager tried to prevent them from mounting the stairs, but Chard brushed him aside. The manager wrung his hands. He had a professional nose for trouble and he smelled it now.

They burst in on Howard who started to say: 'Chard, what is the meaning—?' but Blade cut him short.

'Howard, you hear me now and you hear me good.'

Howard was on his feet, shouting: 'Chard, do something.' He spoke as if he could not believe that Chard would dismiss all difficulties from his path.

'Esmeralda Santiago has been taken too.'

Howard stared at their faces in turn, as if to find there some refutation of this statement.

Frantically, he asked: 'Tell me what goes on here.'

'The answer is Glory,' Blade told him. 'Your partner just turned on you. There's no other explanation. I have concrete proof that Glory fixed for Jim Flaherty to be killed.'

'What kind of proof?' Howard asked.

'The man who did it. Is that enough for you?'

Howard sat down. His face was white.

'My God,' he said. 'What a fool I've been.'

The door opened. They all turned. A tall thin man stood in the open doorway. It was Phil Larson.

'I reckon I heard my boss's name,' he said. His hard cold eyes were on Blade. Harry Simpson slapped his right hand down on his gun butt. The gunman brushed the gesture aside with a motion of his right hand and said: 'Don't touch it, Simpson, or you're a dead man. Now, I have a few words for you all. Mr Glory has gone north.'

Blade said: 'You mean he's run for it?'

Larson ignored the insult. He sniffed once and said: 'He left me in charge. He also left me the women. It ain't my choice, but there ain't nothin' I can do about it. I earned my wages all my life an' I don't mean to change the habit of a lifetime.'

Howard yelped furiously: 'You will release the ladies at once, Larson. Do you hear me?'

'Howard,' Larson said, 'Mr Glory is real mad at you. Maybe it's that daughter of yourn is too durned purty for her own good. Hell, the truth is you-all are to back off from Santiago and you, Blade, you pull out from it. Mr Glory is sure set on havin' the place an' I aim to see he gets it.'

Blade moved forward into the centre of the room and faced the man.

'You're a yellow dog, Larson,' he said softly.

The gunman's eyes widened, his nostrils flared. Rage shook him from head to foot.

'By God,' he said, 'nobody ever said a thing like that to me an' lived.'

Blade said: 'You didn't have the nerve to draw on me at Glory's place and you don't have now.'

'That's a goddam lie an' you know it,' Larson said.

'To prove it,' said Blade, 'you have to draw.'

'It ain't in Mr Glory's interest,' Larson said.

'You'll have to do better than that.'

The simple remark seemed to have an even more profound effect on the gunman than the first insult.

'No call to take advantage, Blade,' he said in the tone of a hurt child. 'You know I'm a man to do his duty. I work for Mr Glory. It ain't in my book to take a side trail.'

Blade said softly and persistently: 'If you were half a man, Phil, if you weren't past it, you'd be willing to take the risk. I know I can draw on you and plant two slugs in your brisket before you can cock your gun. I know it. As sure as you're standing there, I know it. I'm faster and I'm better. There's not a living man can beat me to the draw.'

Larson was white to the lips.

'Shut it, Blade,' he said, 'or I'll gun you down where you stand.'

Blade laughed.

'It's too easy,' he said. 'The word'll get around through your friends that I tricked you or took you by surprise. I want the whole damn world to know I'm the better man. I'll gamble on my speed, Phil. Will you gamble on yours?'

Larson hesitated. There was a terrible silence in the room. Howard drew in shuddering breath.

'Name it,' said Larson finally. His voice was hoarse.

'If you gun me down,' Blade said. 'Santiago, the whole shooting match. Women included. It's yours.'

'If you kill me?' said Larson and licked his dry lips.

'Naturally, the reverse. Your men let the women go.'

The words seemed to hang in the silence of the room.

Larson began: 'I—' and stopped. He looked trapped and wretched, his pride fighting his loyalty. It was as if the battle going on inside him was almost unbearable.

Then he relaxed suddenly as he made his decision.

'All right,' he said. 'I'll make the arrangements. I'll meet you on the street outside in thirty minutes. Not before and not after. Thirty minutes exact. We meet with our guns in leather. We agree we're ready. Then we draw.'

Blade nodded.

Harry Simpson said gently: 'My God.'

Larson half-turned away and stopped to say: 'You're a brave man, Joe, but a damn fool for all that.'

Blade did not speak and the four men in the room listened to the retreating bootheels of the veteran gunman.

Chard remarked: 'I never thought I'd live to see the classic gunfight.'

Howard said: 'You goddam fool, Blade. Now my two lovely girls are lost to me. Go call Larson back. Do some kind of deal with him.'

Blade said: 'I just made the only kind of deal he understands. There was no other way. Hell, do you think I like gunfighting?'

'Thirty minutes,' said Harry Simpson. 'How do we live through a half-hour, not knowing? If you lose me Esmeralda, Blade—'

Howard yelled suddenly: 'This is time for intelligent civilised men to take over. Blade, I'm telling you—'

Chard startled them all by suddenly catching his employer by the sleeve and saying in a voice that shook with fury: 'Mr Howard, you open your stupid mouth once more and I'll knock your teeth down your throat.'

Blade laughed and said: 'That goes for you too, Harry. Now

let's get to work. Larson's no fool and he's going to set us up in some way. Chard, can you get up on the roof opposite with a rifle? Harry, see that dark alleyway yonder? In there with your Winchester. Howard, you man this window. Now, you all listen to what I have to say and you listen good because we can't afford any kind of slip up. Maybe Larson's playing this straight and maybe he isn't. Whatever he does, I aim for us to come out on top.'

He talked for five minutes. Then he asked them if they understood and they nodded. Even Howard seemed to accept the situation.

Then Blade prepared himself for the street.

First, he carefully washed his hands in Howard's basin. Second, he checked his gun with his gloves on so he would get no oil on them. Then, satisfied that the weapon was in good working order, he slid it into the holster at his side and tested it for the ease with which it could be withdrawn. The others watched him in awed silence, realising that they were to be witnesses of a western drama of which they had heard many times, but which they, as most other men, had never seen. As for Blade himself, he seemed strangely calm for a man who might well be about to die. They searched his face for a tell-tale sign of nerves, but found none. They knew then that it took a certain kind of man to face a moment like this and they were not such men.

Chard said: 'A snort of whisky, Mr Blade?'

Blade finished tying his holster down and looked up at him, saying: 'That's kind of you, Mr Chard, but no, this is best done with a clear head.' Now he removed his gloves and tried one draw with his bare hand. It did not seem especially fast, but it seemed to satisfy him. He said: 'Take your positions, gentlemen, and, remember, only shoot if you have to.' He clapped Harry Simpson on the shoulder and added: 'Be careful where you point that damn Winchester, Harry. I'd hate to be shot down by my own side.'

They wished him luck and left the room. Howard stayed near the window, looking out anxiously on to the street.

'Howard,' Blade said, 'there's going to be a whole lot of indiscriminate shooting down there. Don't even flirt with the idea that you can put a shot in between my shoulder blades.'

The millionaire looked scandalised – 'I don't know how you can even think of such a thing.'

Blade grinned and said: 'I think such things all the time. That's why I'm still alive.'

He walked out of the room and went slowly down the stairs. The owner was standing in the lobby with the desk clerk. They turned their pale faces towards him and the owner said: 'Is it true, Mr Blade, you're going out against Phil Larson?' Blade nodded and the man added: 'I guess we're going to see history made.'

Blade didn't quite see what a gunfight on a Laredo street had to do with history. He went out on to the street and looked up and down. It was unusually empty. He pulled the skirt of his coat back behind his holster. The light was poor and uncertain, a treacherous mixture of moonlight and lamplight. Larson, the old hand, would know how to make the best of such a situation. Blade sighed to himself. The answer to all such problems was one bullet put in the right place.

He stood in the centre of the street.

The silence that surrounded him then seemed to swell and swell, pushing its way up and down the street.

At the same time, the silence seemed to press in on him.

He glanced up and saw the moonlight dully touching metal and knew that Chard was in position.

There came a faint sound. It was a man walking up from the lower town. His spur chains made a soft night music. Blade made out the tall angular figure of Captain McNally, the Ranger. For a moment, Blade mistook him for Larson.

The Ranger kept to the south side of the street. He halted a short pistol shot from Blade and called: 'I hear there's going to be a fight, Blade. I'll take your gun.'

From the mouth of the alley came Harry Simpson's voice – 'This is a Winchester looking at you, captain. Take a tip from me and get off the street.'

Blade added his argument to Harry's – 'Do like he says, McNally. This is going to be a case of shooting in self-defence. You won't stop it.'

McNally shrugged and crossed the street. He sat down on the sidewalk and waited. A man appeared from a doorway near him and stood on the sidewalk watching Blade. It was Lee Tolliver.

'Hello, Lee,' Blade said. 'You in this fight or out of it?'

Tolliver said: 'This ain't my fight, Joe. My word on it. I owe you, remember?'

Blade smiled.

A figure appeared indistinctly in the lamplight about a hundred paces east of him.

This was Larson. Blade wanted to laugh. The gunman was going to make a long walk of it, each pace calculated to weaken a little more of the opponent's nerve. The realisation did not make Blade unhappy. He knew that his mind was enjoying the utter calm of pure necessity. If his mind became flurried, he was as good as dead or crippled. If his mind stayed at peace, but permitted itself to be stimulated by the close proximity of danger, he would be left standing, alive, on the street, while this tall master-gunman pacing slowly towards him would be dead.

He heard Larson's words – 'Start the ball any time you want, Joe. I'm comin' to kill you.'

Three paces.

'Any time you want, Joe. It's up to you whether you live or die.'

Three paces.

'It's the speed of your right hand against the speed of my left. Or call it off. It's up to you now, Joe.'

Three paces.

Blade stood very still, looking like a man standing at his ease, nothing like a man about to draw a gun for his life.

'Make your play, Joe or did your guts run out on you?'

Three paces.

There was a patch of lamplight behind Larson's head now, giving him a golden halo around his head, making him look like some avenging angel.

'Just one shot is all it needs, Joe.'

Blade thought: *I believe he genuinely thinks I'm scared.* The suggestion that Larson was underestimating him was solid encouragement.

The halo switched off suddenly. Lamplight from Larson's left struck the side of his face and his left shoulder. The silver conchos on his hat band flickered back the light.

Three paces.

The light changed again. Larson walked into a patch of almost total darkness. But the light jingle of the spur-chains would have guided any bullet of Blade's to its mark.

'You're nearly too late to draw, Joe.'

Blade hurled himself to the left, hitting dirt hard with his shoulder, his right hand smoothly taking the gun from leather and cocking it. He could see the faint reflection of lamplight on Larson's boots and he aimed above it.

Larson had drawn and fired instantly as Blade started the dive. The shot kicked up dirt. The second shot ploughed up dust as Blade rolled. The third shot clipped Blade's elbow as Blade's gun released one shot – the one shot that was necessary in a fight to the death. It took the veteran gunman in the centre of the chest. He swayed backwards under the impact of the heavy slug, put a foot out to steady himself and pitched forward on to his face.

Blade stood up and passed his gun to his left hand. His right arm hung uselessly as the blood dripped from his fingertips.

'Bring out the women, Lee,' he called.

There was a rush of movement from behind Tolliver. Three women ran forward.

Two shots came, close together.

Blade heard a cry from above him and he saw Lee Tolliver with a smoking gun in his hand. He watched Ransome Howard push his head through the open window and then slowly follow it with his thin body. It seemed to hang in mid-air for a moment, then plummeted into the street. All movement seemed to cease. Blade stood there in a daze, wondering how badly he was hit. But suddenly, Tolliver was near and saying: 'I owed you, Joe. The old buzzard was cutting down on you.'

Blade could see June Howard. She appeared to be weeping on Chard's shoulder. How Chard had got down from the roof in that time, he never knew. Maybe he had stood there bleeding and shocked longer than he thought. Already Harry Simpson was across the street and Blade was damned if he didn't see Esmeralda Morales in *his* arms.

On leaden feet, he walked over and looked down at Howard. The bullet had taken him in the heart. He looked up and saw the cold stricken face of Narcissa.

Captain McNally walked quietly into the scene.

'Joe,' he said, 'get that arm fixed and do me a favour. Don't take to long getting out of my bailiwick.'

Narcissa was holding his good arm and saying something about getting him to a doctor.

'Narcissa,' he said, 'I'm sorry.'

Narcissa said: 'I saw him. He was trying to kill you, Joe.'

There's not really a lot more to tell.

Blade had his arm fixed by the doctor and he rode out of Laredo. Maybe he listened to McNally's warning and maybe he did not. Certainly, he was not seen again on the Santiago grant. The irrigation scheme was progressing well. Harry

Simpson seemed to have thrown himself whole-heartedly into the work and had shown himself quite capable of running the whole shooting-match.

About a month after the gunfight in Laredo, Joe Blade was riding into the hills above Santiago with a red-headed woman by his side. They rode to a lonesome canyon on the edge of the Santiago grant and tied their horses among the willows on the edge of a pool there.

They sat on the grass side by side and the woman said: 'Life is full of surprises. There's June suddenly tamed by a quiet man none of us ever really noticed, and I guess she's pretty happy. Whoever thought she'd fall for a man like Chard, Joe?'

'And Esmeralda,' he said, 'whoever thought she'd settle for old Harry Simpson or that Harry would settle for a job like running Santiago.'

She said: 'Joe, was there really ever a piece of Spanish paper?'

He smiled and said: 'Sometimes I think it never existed. Esmeralda never admitted there wasn't, but I guess she didn't dare to, because she thought she had to have something to prove her ownership.'

'Why did my husband want to find Flaherty's killer? Why did he hire you? Though I'm durned glad he did.'

Blade explained: 'He wanted to know who else was after the Spanish script beside himself. Then he found out it was Glory, and after a while he realised he could never beat Glory when it came to a show down. Glory was a Westerner and he played rough – with guns to boot.'

She changed the subject abruptly.

'And why did you settle for me, Joe?'

'Not to put too fine a point on it,' he said, 'I have a sort of talent. All three of you are remarkably beautiful women. But only you are a millionairess.'

She smiled.

'Is that all I am,' she asked, 'a millionairess?'

'No,' he said, 'You are about the most beautiful woman I ever saw. Your lips are perfect and make a promise I can't wait to have made good. Your neck I never saw the like of. As for your figure, why, Narcissa, I reckon it makes me forget I ever pretended to be a gentleman. But, hell, they're all a part of the bonus being paid on *The Laredo Assignment*.'

Also in Hamlyn Paperbacks

Matt Chisholm

THE TUCSON CONSPIRACY

They gambled bloodily with the lives of innocent men and women . . .

They used mayhem and murder to fulfil their ambitions . . .

The prize in their deadly gamble was the Territory of Arizona. Law and order rested in the hands of Joe Blade, lovely Charity Clayton and veteran scout George McMasters. The Tucson Ring had penetrated all walks of life in the Territory. Only two men and a woman stood between them and power.